I0648577

Timothy Walker

Diaries of Rev. Timothy Walker

The first and only minister of Concord, N.H., from his ordination

November 18, 1730, to September 1, 1782

Timothy Walker

Diaries of Rev. Timothy Walker
The first and only minister of Concord, N.H., from his ordination November 18, 1730, to September 1, 1782

ISBN/EAN: 9783337385941

Printed in Europe, USA, Canada, Australia, Japan

Cover: Foto ©Raphael Reischuk / pixelio.de

More available books at **www.hansebooks.com**

DIARIES

OF

REV. TIMOTHY WALKER,

THE FIRST AND ONLY MINISTER OF CONCORD, N. H.,

FROM HIS ORDINATION NOVEMBER 18, 1730,

TO SEPTEMBER 1, 1782.

EDITED AND ANNOTATED

BY

JOSEPH B. WALKER.

CONCORD, N. H.:
IRA C. EVANS, PRINTER, 13 AND 15 CAPITOL ST.
1889.

DIARIES OF THE REV. TIMOTHY WALKER,

THE FIRST AND ONLY MINISTER OF CONCORD, NEW HAMPSHIRE, FROM HIS ORDINATION, NOVEMBER 18, 1730, TO HIS DEATH, SEPTEMBER 1, 1782.

—

PREFATORY NOTE.

The Rev. Timothy Walker, author of the following diaries, was the first minister of Pennycook, now Concord, N. H., and from the organization of its church to his death, a period of fifty-two years, its only one.

He was born in Woburn, Mass., on the 27th day of July, 1705, was graduated at Harvard College in 1725, and settled at Pennycook on the 18th day of November, 1730. This was his first and only settlement. As did his neighbors, he went there to stay, and at once identifying himself with all their interests, he devoted to these the energies of his entire life. He possessed good mental abilities, a good eduation, strong common sense, and marked wisdom. He was not only their spiritual advisor, but their legal and temporal counsellor as well.

His modest salary,* insufficient for his support, was supplemented by the income of the parsonage lands and the farm which was given by the proprietors of the township to their first settled minister. He thus became a farmer as well as minister, and, through this relation, was brought into more intimate sympathy with his people than he might otherwise have been.

His pacific feelings and good sense contributed to the maintenance of friendly relations with the neighboring Indians, liable at any time to be provoked to acts of violence by imaginary grievances or the wiley counsels of the French.

But, pacific as was his disposition, he held firmly to the sacred right of self-defence. When, therefore, some twenty years after his settlement at Pennycook, a company having little existence but upon paper laid claim to the fair town which his people had wrested from the wilderness, he personally championed their cause, and, in the prosecution of

---

* £100 per annum, equal to $130.67 in silver.

appeals from the decisions of the New Hampshire courts, made no less than three voyages to England in their behalf, where he finally obtained, from the King in Council, the redress denied them at home. This struggle lasted about thirteen years.

All through the Revolutionary war he was an ardent patriot. He lived to rejoice at the surrender of Lord Cornwallis, to see the establishment of independence, and the substantial close of the war. He died September 1, 1782.

For a large portion of his life Mr. Walker kept brief diaries of current events. It is to be regretted that most of these have perished. Three, however, have been preserved entire, and fragments of six others. They afford vivid pictures of New Hampshire life on the Indian frontier while the question of English or French supremacy on this continent was being decided and while the inestimable privileges of American independence were being achieved.

J. B. W.

Concord, March 1, 1889.

DIARY OF REV. TIMOTHY WALKER.
1746.

Woodwell's Garrison was taken April 22.[1]
Thomas Cook & als. killed May y[e] 9.[2]
Richard Blanchard scalped June 11.[3]
Bishop was captivated June 25.
Jon[a] Bradley & als. killed Aug: 11.[4]
Easterbrook killed Nov[r] 10.[5]

Killed, 8.   Captivated, 12.   Died of his wounds, 1.

---

1. Woodwell's garrison was in Hopkinton, a short distance from Contoocookville, near the point where the road to Tyler's Bridge branches from the main road.

2. A Boscawen man, killed on Clay Hill just above the Plain.

3. A Canterbury man.

4. Jonathan Bradley of Exeter, Samuel Bradley and Obadiah Peters of Concord, John Lufkin of Kingston, and John Bean of Brentwood, who were massacred on the road to Hopkinton, about a mile from Concord. A granite obelisk now marks the locality and commemorates the event.

5. He was a Hopkinton man, and was shot by an Indian near the watering trough at the foot of Rum Hill.

JANUARY.

1, D.   Very cold.   Remained at Woburn.
2, D.   At night went and lodged at Brother
        Walkers.[6]
3, D.   Sat out homeward.   Lodged at Mr. Flaggs.[7]
4, D.   Arrived home.
5, D.   Preached all day at home.
6, D.   Visited over ye River.
7, D.   Moderate weather.
8, D.   Ditto.
9, D.   Snowed and then turned to rain.   Visited
        with Mr. Stevens over ye River.
10, D. Cleared up very cold.   Capt. Goffe dined
        at our house.[8]
11, D. A very cold morning.   Went up to Con-
        toocook.
12, D. Preached all day there.   Mr. Page preached
        here.   Returned home at night.
13, D. Visited Capt. Eastman[9] just returned from
        Boston with news of ye Pretender's suc-
        cess in Scotland.[10]
15, D. Capt. Eastman and wife dined at our house.
        Remainder of ye week tarried at home.
        This week has been very warm.
19, D. Preached all day at home.

6.   Samuel Walker, of Woburn, Mass.

7.   Rev. Ebenezer Flagg, a classmate of Mr. Walker and for sixty years the pastor of the church in Chester.

8.   Afterwards known as Col. John Goffe, a prominent citizen of Amherst.

9.   Capt. Ebenezer Eastman, one of the most enterprising citizens of Concord.

10.   Charles Edward, son of James Francis Edward Stuart, grandson of James 2d and claimant of the British throne.   The success mentioned above was, probably, the defeat of the English army at Preston Pans, September 21, 1745, and the capture of Carlisle, Nov. 26th of the same year.

20. D. Visited Mr. A. Whittemore being sick of fever.[11]

22, D. Visited at Deacon Merrill's.[12]

25, D. A warm snow. This week; also has been very warm.

26. D. Preached all day at home. Cleared up very blustering. Y⁰ new snow being about mid leg deep drifted very much.

27, D. Warm again.

28, D. Warm. Began to hall Fort Timber.[13]

27 D. Moderate yᵉ rest of this Week.

N : B : 3ᵈ day pd. Mr. Philips all yᵗ I owed him except 0—13—4. and Wm. Pudney's order of 3—00—00. Sum Total—or what I owe him is 3—13—4.

FEBRUARY.

1, D. A. M. Snowed. Mr. Stevens[14] came and lodged at our house.

2. D. He preached here and baptized Abraham, yᵉ son of Abᵐ Colby; Ebenʳ. yᵉ son of Sampson Colby, and Abigail yᵉ daughter of James Abbot Junior. I Preached at Contoocook.

3. D. At night it hail a great deal.

4, D. Visited at Mr. Lovejoys[14½]. Yᵉ rest of yᵉ week very warm.

11. Rev. Aaron Whittemore, first minister of Pembroke, ordained March 12, 1737.

12. John Merrill, the first deacon of the Concord church, against whom the first suit for ejectment was brought in the celebrated Bow controversy.

13. This timber was for the garrison built around Mr. Walker's house this year.

14. Rev. Phineas Stevens, first Pastor of the Boscawen church, ordained Oct. 8, 1740.

14½. Probably Capt. Henry Lovejoy, who had a grist mill at West Concord, and afterwards a forge used in the manufacture of bar iron.

8, D.   It seemed to thicken up for a storm of rain but cleared away again.

9. D.   Preached all day at home, and baptized Isaac ye son of Benjn Abbot and Sarah ye daughter of Joseph Pudney.

10. D. Eben Hall came to live with me. We sledded wood.

11, D. Ditto.

12. D. At night Col. Rolfe[15] returned from Newbury. It was a cold night for this moderate winter.

13. D. Col. Rolfe dined at our house.

14, D. Warm again. Snowed a little.

15. D. Ditto.

16, D. Preached all day at home.

17, D. Fair weather. Received a letter from Woburn.

19, D. Visited with Col. Rolfe over ye River. At night he lodged at our house.

       N. B.   From the 8 instant to ye 20 inclusive got home about 30 loads of wood for my years stock.

21, D. A very cold, blustering day.

22, D. Y^e weather moderated. Looked like rain but turned to a spitting snow.

23, D. Preached all day at home, and baptized Ezekiel ye son of Tim. Walker Junior.

24. D. Extraordinary cold for ye season. Visited at Col. Rolfe's. Pd. Mr. Simonds for my barrel of cyder.

25, D. Cold. Carried my wife up to Mr. Lovejoy's a visiting.[15½]

---

15. Col. Benjamin Rolfe, the largest landholder of Concord, and one of its most prominent citizens. He subsequently married one of Mr. Walker's daughters.

15½. Neighbourhood visiting was vigorously pursued in olden times. Mothers frequently carried their infants to tea parties, and

26, D.   Received yͤ news of yͤ King of Prussia
          having made peace with yͤ Queen of
          Hungary.[16]
          Yͤ rest of the week cold whilst yͤ Satur-
          day and then yͤ weather moderated.

MARCH.

2, Day   Preached all day at home.
3, "   Capt. Goffe was at our house.
4, "   Carried my wife a visiting down to Col.
          Rolfe's. Wind still strong at North
          West for a fortnight.
5   "   Weather moderated. Visited with my
          wife at Uncle Walker's. Married Jacob
          Shute and Abigail Evans. Now warm.
          Spring-like weather.
6   "   Fetched a load of rails from Tim.———
7   "   Sledded dung overto yͤ Island.
8   "   Hauled off my logs from my plowed land.
9   "   Preached at Contoocook. Mr. Stevens
          preached for me and baptized Peter yͤ
          son of Nathˡ Rix. A North East
          storm which lasted 3 or 4 days.
11 "   Measured (?) Jos. Pudney's hay.
13 "   A general Fast. Preached all day.
14 "   A warm, pleasant day.
15 "   A N: East storm. Very uncomfortable
          weather.
16 "   Yͤ storm continued. Very miry going.
          Preached all day at home.

when putting on their wraps to return home, they laid them for a
moment somewhat promiscuously upon the bed. This practice sometimes led to inadvertent changes, a matter of little consequence,
Judge Walker used to remark, as the mistake could always be righted
at the next meeting, sure to come a few days after.

16. Frederick the Great and Maria Theresa.

20	Day	Went over yᵉ River upon yᵉ ice. It grew very rotten. Capt. Stevens[17] came up and lodged at our house.
21	"	I settled accts. with him for boarding soldiers to yᵉ 25th of Feb. past. N. B. Yᵉ week past has been cold for yᵉ season.
22	"	Preached all day at home.
23	"	Yᵉ weather moderated.
24	"	Wife in company with her brother, James Burbeen,[17½] sat out for Woburn. Crossed yᵉ Ferry upon yᵉ ice which was very weak.
25	"	Went over the river.
26	"	Haled in some logs into Capt. Eastman's mill. N. B. 25 D. Began to hew timber for my East Buttery [?]
28	"	Capt. Stevens sat out home.
29	"	Moderate weather. Capt. Stevens returned to execute some new orders.
30	"	Preached at Suncook. Mr. Whittemore preached here and baptized Sarah yᵉ daughter of Nathan Stevens.

APRIL.

1	Day	Cut thro yᵉ ice and crossed Horse Pond with a canoe.
2	"	Began to cross plow at yᵉ Island.[18]
3	Day	Ditto.

---

17. Probably Capt. Phineas Stevens, a celebrated Indian fighter and one of the first settlers of Charlestown.

17½. The grandson of John Burbeen, of Woburn, Mass., who was a Scotchman and the first Anglo-American ancestor of the family of that name. This name, as a sirname, is now supposed to be extinct in this country.

18. Horse-Shoe Island, which constituted a part of Mr. Walker's farm.

4 Day.   Was beat off by ye rains w^h come in pretty great plenty.

5   "   Y^e freshet rose considerably; cold, windy.

6   "   Preached all day at home. Administered ye Sacrament. Baptized Nathl, ye son of Judah Trumball.

7   "   Snowed some.

8   "   More moderate.

9   "   Went to Contoocook with Col. Rolfe.

10 "   Burnt my lower pasture.

11 "   Showery. Col. Rolfe sat out for Newbury.

12 "   Very warm. Began to plow over ye River.

13 "   Showery. Preached all day at home. Baptized Miriam ye daughter of Lieutenant Jere. Stickney. At night rained hard.

14 "   Sowed my barley.

15 & 16 Day   Dripping weather.

17 Day   Carried my Team over ye River to plow my land there.

18 & 19 Day   Tarried at home. The Floods, notwithstanding ye many threatenings were not great this year as yet.

20 "   Preach all day at home, and baptized Jeremiah ye son of Stephen Farrington.

22 "   Y^e Indians took Woodwell's Garrison.

23 "   Sat out to meet my wife. Lodged at Mr. Moore's.

24 "   Met Col. Rolfe. P. M. Went to Wilmington.

25 "   Went to Boston to carry news of ye Indian mischief.

26 "   Return to Woburn.

27 "   Kept Sabbath there.

28 "   Sold my place there. P. M. Went to Litchfield.

29 Day. Returned home.

30 " Tarried at home.

N: B: Y^e 6th day admitted Nathl Abbot and wife ye full communion.

MAY.

2. Day   Visited over ye River.[18⅓]

3 " Tarried at home.

4 " Preached all day at home. Jos. Eastman. Tertius, owned ye covenant. In
the night we had tidings of mischief
being done about sunset at Contoocook
by ye Indians. Thomas Cook & als.
killed.

5 " Col. Rolfe sat out to Boston.

7 " A considerable Frost.

7 & 8 Day   Planted my corn.

9 Day   Went up to Rattlesnake for stone.

10 " My Pasture fence built up.

11 " Preached all day and administered the
Sacrament.

10 " Turned ye cows into my pasture.

12 " Got hands and mended my pasture fence.

13 " Col Blanchard and als. came up.

14 " They dined here.

15 " Returned to Suncook.

16 " Very warm.

17 " Nathl Rolfe returned from Newbury.

18 " Preached all day at home.

19 " Mrs. Rolfe sat out for Newbury.

22 " Married William Pudney and Hannah
Bryar.

23&24 " Joseph Pudney & als. built their chim-
neys.

25 " Preached all day at home.

18⅓. East Concord.

26 Day   Dined at Col. Rolfe's.
27 "   At night Col. Rolfe came and lodged at our house.
28 "   Election. Joseph Pudney and Ob^h Foster moved into ye houses.[19]
29 "   Sold my colt to Mr. Leonard Harriman.
30 "   Mr. Nathl Rolfe sat out for Newbury.
31 "   Very warm.

N. B. The fore part of ye last week of May was a very cold season.

JUNE.

1 Day.   Preached all day at home. Baptized Saml ye son of Wm. Curry.
2 "   Capt. Melvin[19½] came up and brought news of an expedition to Canada.[20]
3 "   Breakfasted at Col. Rolfe's.
4 "   He sat out for Boston.
5 "   Visited over ye River.
6 "   Warm.
7 "   Mr. Stevens returned from Andover.
8 "   Preached all day. Baptized David ye son of Jos: Eastman ye 3d. Administered ye Sacrament.
9 "   Went over ye River.

---

19. Small houses erected within the walls of Mr. Walker's garrison. The families assigned to this fortification, May 15, 1746, by the committee appointed by Gov. Benning Wentworth, "for settling the garrisons in the frontier towns and plantations" of New Hampshire, were those of Capt. John Chandler, Abraham Bradley, Samuel Bradley, John Webster, Nathaniel Rolfe, Joseph Pudney, Isaac Walker, Jr., and Obadiah Foster.

19½. Capt. Eleazer Melvin, of Concord, Mass., a survivor of the battle at Pigwacket and a soldier in King George's war.

20   The expedition was supported by the several colonies as far south as Virginia. The New Hampshire House of Representatives assembled on the third day of June and decided a day or two after to coöperate with their sister colonies in the enterprise.

10	Day	Soaking rain. Sat out about 200 cabbage plants.
11	"	Cleared up. Benjⁿ Blanchard, of Canterbury, was scalped by ye indians.

10 Day   Soaking rain. Sat out about 200 cabbage plants.

11 "   Cleared up. Benjn Blanchard, of Canterbury, was scalped by y[e] indians.

12 "   Our Town was universally alarmed by y[e] hearing some guns discharged in y[e] woods. At night Col. Rolfe returned from Boston.

13 "   Teams arrived home.

14 "   Extreme hot.

15 "   Turned up cool. Preached all day at home.

16 "   Moulded[21] my Island Corn.

17 "   We heard abundance of great guns at Portsmouth at night. Married Eben Hall to Dorcas Abbot.

19 "   Capt. Stevens came up.

20 "   A most plentiful rain after a sore drought.

21 "   Cleared up.

22 "   Preached all day at home. Baptized Isaac y[e] son of Isaac Waldron.

23 "   Built y[e] Tailor's chimney.[22]

24 "   Wm. Stickney brought up my new gun,[23] and my mare from Andover.

25 "   Visited over y[e] River.

27 "   Showery. Carried my wife down to Uncle Walker's.

28 "   Showery. N. B. 25 D.—Bishop was captivated by y[e] Indians.

---

21. "Moulded" was synonymous with "half-hilled." The three successive hoeings of a corn crop were denominated weeding, moulding and hilling.

22. Isaac Walker, familiarly called Tailor Walker, from his occupation. He had a temporary dwelling within the inclosure of Mr. Walker's garrison.

23. Tradition says that Mr. Walker had the best gun in the parish and that, during times of danger, when his people went to meeting, this stood beside him in the pulpit while he conducted the services.

29 Day   Preached at home. Baptized Jemima ye daughter of Edward Abbot, and Mehitabel ye daughter of Amos Eastman.

30 "   An alarm over ye River on account of Indians being seen.

JULY.

1 Day.   News from Newbury of Admiral Warren's[25] arrival. Dorcas Hall saw an Indian at night. George Hall lay abroad and saw six Indians.[26]

4 "   Thomas Eastman arrived home from Cape Breton.

5 "   Attended ye funeral of Lieu^t Stickney's child.

6 "   Preached all day at home.

7 "   Some small showers. Visited over ye River.

8 "   Extreme hot.

9 "   Ditto. Capt. Eastman returned from Cape Breton.

10 "   A publick fast to implore ye divine blessing upon ye Canada expedition.[27] Preached all day at home,

11 "   Visited over ye River. Very hot.

12 "   Showering in some places.

13 "   Preached all day at home.

14 "   Tarried at home.

15 "   In company with Capt. Eastman and others sat out for Woburn. Lodged at Capt. Copp's.

---

25. Sir Peter Warren, commodore of the British squadron, engaged at the siege of Louisburg, in 1745.

26. During hostilities between England and France, incursions of Indians were liable to occur at any time and a sharp watch for them was maintained.

27. The plan of this expedition was never executed.

16 Day   Went to Woburn.

18   "   Went to Boston.   Returned to Woburn at night.

20   "   Preached P : M : at Woburn Precinct.

22   "   Went to Boston again.

23   "   Went to Wilmington.

24   "   Lodged at Capt Baldwin's.

25   "   Arrived home.

27   "   Preached all day at home.   N : B : 24 D. Night rained considerably.

30   "   Capt. Eastman and others returned from Boston.

N. B.   24 D.   Reckoned with my brother Samuel Walker and for yᵉ 300 pounds old Tenour he has of mine he accounted for in the following manner. 100 he let Christopher Temple have. 100 he gave me up my bond and note to him £50 each. for yᵉ other hundred he produced my note to Col. Rolfe.

AUGUST.

1 Day.   Went to see Capt. Eastman newly returned from Boston who paid me £30 upon account of Leonard Harriman.

3   "   Rained somewhat. Preached all day. Baptized Samuel yᵉ son of Patrick Garvin.

4   "   Went to Contoocook and fetched my ox from thence [there ?].

6   "   Went in yᵉ evening to Lovejoy's mill.

8   "   A very great shower.

9   "   Spread my flax. Extreme hot.

10   "   Preached at home.

11   "   Jonᵃ Bradley and als. were killed by the Indians.

12   "   Joseph Pudney's wife was buried.

14   "   A publick Thanksgiving for yᵉ suppression of yᵉ Scotch Rebellion.

15 Day   Got up ye great boat and began to get over my English corn.

16   "   Got over all my English corn.—Andover men came up to guard us.[30]

17   "   Preached all day at home.

18   "   Mighty foggy weather the most of this week, especially ye 3 first working days so y^t but little business could be done.

23   "   I had six hands to mow for me.[31]

24   "   Preached all day at home.

25   "   Raked my hay.

26   "   Carted 4 loads.

27   "   Sat out for Andover. Lodged at Capt. Stevens.

28   "   Went to Woburn.

29   "   Went to Boston.

30   "   Put in a petition for help against ye indians.

31   "   Kept Sabbath at ye new meeting house, Woburn.[32]

SEPTEMBER.

1 Day   Almost lay still with my boil.

2   "   Ditto. Stormy.

3   "   Went to Boston to obtain a grant of 20 men.[33]

---

30. Massachusetts repeatedly sent small bodies of soldiers to guard the frontiers. New Hampshire did the same, but the people of Concord were not favorites at Portsmouth, and the town was never allowed a representation in the assembly under the Provincial Government.

31. Much of the grass cut on the interval at that time was a wild grass (Andropogon Virginiensis and A. scoparius) which does not mature until the middle of August. It is of inferior quality as compared with cultivated grasses. The first species sometimes attains a height of over seven feet.

32. The meeting-house of Woburn, Mass., Precinct, now Burlington, erected in 1732.

33. These doubtless were to guard the frontier.

4 Day	Gov'. Shirleys wife was buried. At night returned to Woburn.
5&6 "	Tarried there.
7 "	Preached half of ye day for Mr. Clap.[34]
8 "	Went to Andover.
9 "	From thence to Dunstable. Lodged at Col. Blanchard's.[35]
10 "	Sat out homeward with a company from Billerica.
11 "	Arrived home.
12&13 D	Tarried at home.
14 Day	Preached all day at home.
15 "	A false alarm. Went up to Dresser's for apples.
16 "	Capt. Stevens arrived here with news of a French Fleet.[35½]
17 "	Showery.
18 "	Went out into the woods a scouting.[36]
19 "	My brother and ye Billerica men sat out homeward.
20 "	Tarried at home. N: B: 14 D. Baptized Eleanor ye daughter of Eben' Eastman Junior and Sarah ye daughter of James Peters. At night visited some sick children and baptized Edward ye son of Joseph Ordway.
21 "	Preached all day at home.
22 "	Y^e news of a French invasion revived.
23 "	Went out with Capt. Stevens to Hales Town.[38]

34. Rev. Supply Clapp, first pastor of Woburn Precinct Church.

35. Col. Joseph Blanchard was an able officer in the French and Indian wars.

35½. This fleet caused great alarm but did no harm. It was on the northern coast but a short time. A part of the vessels were wrecked and the rest returned to France.

36. Like other able bodied men he took his turn at scouting.

38. Incorporated in 1764, as Weare.

24 Day   Returned home.
25   "   Carted my Island corn.
26   "   Tarried at home.
27   "   Ditto.
28   "   Preached all day at home. Baptized Peter
            ye son of George, Mr. Osgood's servant.[39]
30   "   Visited over ye River with Capt. Stevens.

N: B: Capt Stevens came to board here ye 17 D.

OCTOBER.

1 to 4 Day The remainder of this week gathered my
            Hales Point Corn.
 5 Day   Preached all day. Administered the Sac-
            rament. Baptized Step^n ye son of Step^n
            Hoit.
 6   "   Tarried at home.
 7   "   Visited over ye River.
 8   "   Attended ye funeral of ye child of Jam^s
            Peters.
10   "   A storm.
11   "   Attended ye funeral of Deacon George
            Abbot's[40] child.
12   "   Preached all day at home.
13   "   Picked up stones at Rattlesnake Hill.
14   "   Snowed.
15   "   Capt. Stevens and Judith went away.
16   "   Visited over ye River.
18   "   There fell snow 6 inches deep.
19   "   Preached all day at home.
20   "   Burt came here as a soldier. Visited over
            ye River. The snow began to run
            away.

---

39. Slavery existed in New Hampshire under British rule, and
was never abolished by the Legislature. There were 158 slaves in
the state in 1790.
40. The fourth deacon of the Rumford church.

21 Day   Very warm, pleasant weather for ye season, and so remained ye most of this week. The snow all went away.

25 "   Sent John with my team for a load of candlewood.[41]

26 "   Preached all day at home. Baptized Ephraim ye Son of Dr. Carter.[42]

27 "   Turned my cattle over to ye Middle Interval. N: B: Last night killed a cow. Weighed ℔75 per quarter. Hide weighed 43℔.

29 "   Jos. Farnum helped me burn up logs upon ye Island. A——is out for never was a—— night of finer weather at this time of year than ye last of this month.

NOVEMBER.

1 Day   Began to cross plow. Attended ye funeral of Joseph Hall's daughter.

2 "   Preached all day at home. Administered ye Sacrament. Baptized Stephen ye son of George Abbot.

3 "   Sat out for Woburn in company with Mr. Abra^m Bradley. Lodg^d at Mr. Richard's.

4 "   Pd Mr. Richards [?] for 2 bushels Salt. Went to Woburn and tarried in town ye rest of ye week. Generally very cold. I preached at ye 3d Parish in Woburn.[43]

10 "   Received of Abra^m Bradshaw £300 old ten^r. of w^e see vacant page of this Almanack. 10 ye Indians killed——Esterbrook.

---

41. A splinter of pitch wood was often used instead of a candle. Hence the name.

42. Dr. Ezra Carter, the first regular physician in Concord.

43. This parish was composed of seceders from the first parish, and had but a temporary existence.

11 Day   At night lodged at Brother Walker's.[44]
12 "   Lodged at Brother Wyman's.[45]
13 "   Lodged at Capt. Mitchell's.
14 "   Arrived home with Judith Wyman.
15 "   Began a long storm.
16 "   Preached all day at home. Baptized
          Abner ye son of Jos. Farnham. Con-
          tinued stormy.
17 "   Visited at Capt. Eastman's.
18 "   Began to snow at night. Snowed consid-
          erably.
20 "   Our soldiers were dismissed.[46]
21 & 22 Day   Moderate weather. 22 D. Some of
          Capt Goffe's[47] men arrived at Pen-
          nicook.
23 Day   Preached all day at home.
24 "   Esqr Little arrived here from Haverhill.
27 "   Thanksgiving. Preached all day at home.
28 "   Capt. Goffe's men went away, and carried
          5 days provisions.
30 "   Preached all day at home. Baptized
          Henry ye son of Henry Lovejoy.

DECEMBER.

1 Day   Heard ye news of a cessation of hostil-
          ities.[48]
2 "   Visited over ye River with my wife.
3 "   Killed my hogs.
5 "   Bought 3 sheep of Lieut. Stickney.
6 "   Very warm it has been in general this
          fall.

---

44. Samuel Walker, of Wilmington, Mass.
45. His brother-in-law, Capt. Jesse Wyman, of Woburn, Mass.
46. Soldiers who had been stationed at Concord to guard the frontier.
47. Afterwards Col. John Goffe.
48. Settled peace was not secured until Oct. 18, 1748, by the treaty of Aix La Chapelle.

7 Day   Preached all day at home.

8   "   Visited Col. Rolfe being sick.

9   "   Went into yᵉ woods. Lodged there.[49]

10   "   Snowed somewhat and then turned to rain. We had a very ―― time.

12   "   Yᵉ coldest this winter.

13   "   Continued very cold.

14   "   Preached all day at home.

15   "   Went to mill with a hand sled.[50]

16   "   Yᵉ weather somewhat moderate.

18   "   Yᵉ cold yᵉ renewed yᵉ signs of thaw. Foul weather all turns to cold. So ends yᵉ week.

19   "   At night Edward Wyman Junior arrived here.

21   "   Preached all day at home.

22   "   Bought two deer skins for brother Wyman.

23   "   Very windy. A cold week.

27   "   Yᵉ cold somewhat abated. Snowed a little.

28   "   Preached all day at home. Baptized Abigail yᵉ daughter of Deacon Morrill and Dorothy yᵉ daughter of Lieut. Nathˡ Abbot.

30   "   Haled logs off my plow land.

31   "   Went to Canterbury. Bought a negro wench of Capt. Clough,[51] for wᶜ I am to give him £140. Received of Jere Bradley £―17―00―00. Evil communications corrupt good manners.

1747.

JANUARY.

1 Day   Gave Capt. Clough note for my Negro to be paid yᵉ first day of June next.

---

49. At the mast camp.
50. To the mill at West Concord.
51. Captain Clough of Canterbury.

2 Day   It snowed hard.
3 "   Very cold.
4 "   Preached all day at home. Very cold
        and snowed.

[On a separate page of Mr. Walker's diary for
1746, is recorded the following account of boarding
soldiers sent to help guard the town, viz:]

My account of
boarding soldiers since Feb. 25th, 1745–6.

Feb. 25.   Trull went home and carried two days
provisions with him.

March yᵉ 1st, P: M: he returned and Tarried
whilst yᵉ 8th before dinner and then went away the
same day after dinner.

Wyman came and tarried whilst Tuesday the 25th.
after dinner and then went home yᵉ same day before
dinner.

Clerk Roberts came here and in yᵉ afternoon we
fitted him out with six days provisions for a scout.

24 D.   Lodged Whittemore and gave him supper
and breakfast.

April yᵉ 1. P: M: Pett came here to board and
tarried whilst August yᵉ 2d.

Sept. 17.   Capt Stevens came here and went away
Octo. yᵉ 15.

Burt came and tarried whilst Novʳ 20 and then
was dismissed.

1748.

October 27.   Mr. W. attended yᵉ funeral of his
aged mother-in-law.

1749.

January 7.   Ben. Eastman and family moved up
here.

March.   Pd Sam. Little for making clock case.

May 7.   Abigail, second wife of Jacob Shute. ad.
full com.   She was widow Evans, mother of Jno.

July 2. Sampson Colby and wife ad. full com.

August 29. Bot chair.*

October 10. Preached to Convention at Dover.

1750.

April 8. Ben. Eastman and wife admitted into ye church.

June 24. Sarah Abbot ad. to full com.

October 7. Received Jonathan Straw and wife into our church.

1757.

January 27. Richard Herbert married to Hannah Hall.

October 16. Both owned ye covenant.

November 20. Jona. bap.

1764.

JANUARY.

Sun. 1st of January. New Year's day. Moderate weather. Preached. Baptized Abigail——of Enoch Webster and Mary——of Jona. Merrill.

Mon. 2. Very cold. Matrimonio conjunxi[1] David Gage and Hannah Osgood.

Tues. 3. Very cold. Mr. Gale mended my chains.

Wed. 4. Y^e weather moderated. Visited ye child of James Clements. It was dead before I arrived.

Thurs. 5. Snowed moderately. Attended ye funeral of James Clement's child. Killed 4 hogs.[2]

---

* A vehicle on two wheels, designed for the accommodation of one person, later known as a "gig." This was the first one brought to Concord.

1. Mr. Walker kept up his knowledge of the classics and was accustomed, occasionally, to fit boys for college.

2. Like all country ministers of his time, Mr. W. obtained a part of his support from his farm. While the weights of his swine killed this year may seem light to a farmer of the present day, they were, doubtless, a fair average of those of an hundred years ago.

Weight of my 1st hog 165 lbs;
$$\begin{array}{lll} \text{2d} & \text{"} & 195 & \text{"} \\ \text{3d} & \text{"} & 292 & \text{"} \\ \text{4th} & \text{"} & 227 & \text{"} \end{array}$$

$$\underline{\qquad}$$
879 "

Frid. 6. Cleared up cold. Sledded logs.

Sat. 7. Continued cold.

Sun. 8. Baptiz[d] Benj[a] of Benj[a] Emery and Elizabeth of Eben[r] Griffin. In evening visited Col[o]. Rolfe.[1] Heard the good news of an accommodation with y[e] Indians.

Mon. 9. Y[e] mast team[2] sat out. Cold. My children visited Col[o] Rolfe.

Tues. 10. Continued cold. Sledded logs for my fence.[3] Y[e] coldest night w[h] has been.

Wed. 11. Weather a little moderated. Visited Col[o] Rolfe. On my return, bought a moose skin of ——— Courser for which I am to pay J[o] Chandler Junior £16–10–00.

Thur. 12. Sledded logs for my fence.

1. Col. Benjamin Rolfe, who graduated at Harvard College in 1727, was one of the early proprietors and most influential citizens of Concord. In 1764, he built the house now occupied by the Rolfe & Rumford Asylum, and soon after married Sarah, the oldest daughter of Mr. Walker. Col. Rolfe died in 1771, and his widow subsequently became the wife of Benjamin Thompson, now known as Count Rumford.

2. The furnishing of masts to the ship builders of the coast towns was, for many years, an important business in Concord. Their transportation to the river bank, whence they were floated to their destination, required very large teams, some of which numbered twenty yoke of oxen. Many were collected and rolled into the Contoocook at a place called the "mast yard." Hence came the name of that locality.

3. Fences were often made of whole logs piled one above another upon short blocks between them, and sometimes of split rails supported by morticed posts. Chestnut was a favorite timber for the latter, on account of its easy rift and durability.

Frid. 13. A fine, moderate day. Maj[r] How of New Ipswich came to advise about settling upon y[e] L[ds.] reserved Land. At night Capt Hudson & Mr. N. Rolfe arrived here.

Sat. 14. Appearance of a thaw. Dined at Col[o] Rolfe's in company with Capt. Hudson & Mr. Rolfe.

Sun. 15. A very pleasant day. Preached all day.

Mon. 16. My team sledded fencing stuff. Capt. Hudson and Mr. Rolfe dined at our house.

Tues. 17. Jan. Capt. Hudson took his departure. My team sledded logs. At night Prince[1] with one yoke of oxen went into y[e] mast camp.

Wed. 18. Mr. Webster[2] hauled his great mast at night. Mr. Cotton came & lodged here on his way to Starkstown.[3]

Thurs. 19. Went with Mr. Tim[o] Bradley to find clapboard timber. It thawed very much, then turned cold.

Frid. 20. Moderately cold & clear. At night Prince returned from masting.

Sat. 21. Went to Canterbury in order to change with Mr. Foster.[4] P: M: News came of Reuben Morrill's being killed by the fall of a tree.

Sun. 22. Preached at Canterbury. Mr. Foster preached for me. He baptized Sarah,[5] of Ezekiel Carter. Returned home in y[e] evening.

---

1. Prince was a slave belonging to Mr. Walker. He was subsequently given his freedom and went to Andover, Mass., and afterwards to Woburn, where he died. The bill of sale given to Mr. W. has been preserved and reads as follows :

"Woburn, July 10, 1751.

For value received. I have this day sold to Mr. Timothy Walker a negro boy, named Prince, which I have owned for some time past.

RUTH HAYWARD."

2. Lieut. John Webster, a famous mast master in his day.

3. Starkstown, now Dunbarton.

4. Rev. Abiel Foster, pastor of the Canterbury church from 1761 to 1779. He was subsequently much in public life and a member of Congress.

5. It seems to have been common for a minister, when preaching

Mon. 23. Dined at Col° Rolfe's. P. M. Attended yᵉ meeting of yᵉ inhabitants to choose assessors.[1]

Tues. 24. Snowed about 3 inches deep. Cleared up with a North West wind.

Wed. 25. Capt. McMillen[2] dined here. Visited yᵉ child of Stephen Farrington sick of yᵉ throat disease.

Thurs. 26. Dined at Capt. McMillen's.

Frid. 27. Attended yᵉ funeral of Stephen Farrington's child.

Sat. 28. A pleasant day. Prince sledded logs for fence. Towards night it turned up cold.

Sun. 29. Preached all day. A very moderate day.

Mon. 30. Lot Colby paid me £24–10–00. in full for 4 barrels of cider. £12–00–00 towards his rate for this year.

Tues. 31. Sent my team & brot 960 long shingles[3] from the mast swamp as far as Tim° Bradleys. My team stopped there all night. Signs of rain.

FEBRUARY.

Wed. 1st of Feb. My team brot 900 long shingles. Arrived home about 9 o' the clock. Lamed one of my oxen.

on an exchange, to baptize children of the Parish to which he was temporarily ministering.

1. There is a blank in the Concord town records from 1749 to 1767, owing, doubtless, to the want of a town government during the Bow Controversy.

2. Capt. Andrew McMillen came to this country from Ireland, and for many years was a prominent citizen of Concord. He was a soldier in the last French and Indian war and was present at the destruction of the Indian village of St. Francois in 1759. He removed to Conway in 1774.

3. Long shingles were unshaved, riven shingles, about five or six inches wide and six feet long. They were laid upon purloins, without an underboarding, and were lapped upon one another at the ends and sides.

Thurs. 2. Fell about 6 inches of snow. y^n cleared up moderate.

Frid. 3. Fetched my 900 long shingles from Mr. Tim^o Bradleys.

Sat. 4. My team brot 63 rails from Jon^a Chase's. P. M. Attended ye funeral of Danl Flanders' child.

Sun. 5. A fine, moderate day. Preached all day.

Mon. 6. Disordered with a cold. Visited Col^o Rolfe.

Tues. 7. Dined with wife at Lieut. Hazeltines. P. M. Began to snow pretty hard.

Wed. 8. Cleared up. Sledded logs. Sent Edward Abbot ½ Johannes.[1] Sus pep^t.

Thurs. 9. Mr. Blunt[2] visited me. Sledded logs.

Frid. 10. Prince cleaned about 16 bush^{ls} wheat. Lent Mr. Gale 2 dollars Black pep't.

Sat. 11. Mr. Gale returned me ye 2 borrowed dollars.

Sun. 12. A very warm day. Preached. In ye evening visited Col^o Rolfe.

Mon. 13. Col^o Rolfe gave me a Johannes in ye room of that I gave my son by his order so that I have now 3 Johan^s of his or ye Proprietor's money.

Tues. 14. Changed a heifer with Ensign Walker for a steer. Am to give a dollar to boot.

A very great thaw. Capt. Page[3] lodged with me.

Wed. 15. Continued warm. Sold my quarter of ye cider mill for 8 days work to Farrington. He paid me £24—00—00 for son &c, and £1—00—00 over. N. B. I drew an order on Ed. Presson, dated Feb. 1, to pay Wm. Moore £244—10—00 which is to come out of said Presson's note.

---

1. A Portuguese gold coin of the value of about eight dollars. The name was often contracted into *joe*.

2. Probably Rev. John Blunt, minister of New Castle.

3. Capt. Caleb Page, of Dunbarton.

Thurs. 16. Continued warm. Matrimo° conjunxi Nath¹ Merrill and Anna Walker.

Frid. 17. Attended the marriage entertainment at Deacon Merrill's.

Sat. 18. Prince cleared up 23 bush⁸ of oats. Capt. Gilman and Mr. Barrett visited me. The week has been so moderate that it has carried away most of yᵉ snow. Mr. Scales Junior¹ came to see us.

Sun. 19. Preached. Baptiz⁰ Ruth—of Reuben Abbot.

Mon. 20. Snowed a little and then turned to rain.

Tues. 21. Team sledded logs. Matrimon° junxi Nath¹ Hutchins and Mehitable Ordway.

Wed. 22. Capts. Page, Stark and their wives dined with us.

Thur. 23. Dined at Col° Rolfe's, with Page. In yᵉ evening Major Rogers² arrived.

Frid. 24. Major Rogers dined with us, and Mr. Paul Burbeen³ arrived.

Sat. 25. Cros⁰ Abᵐ Bradley's rates⁴ and paid him £8 cash. Am to pay his father £1, which is yᵉ whole of his due for making long shingles for my barn.

---

1. Mr. Stephen Scales, son of Rev. James Scales, minister of Hopkinton.

2. Major Robert Rogers, the celebrated ranger.

3. Paul Burbeen, then of Woburn, Mass., was a nephew of Mr. Walker's wife. He was a soldier in the French war, serving under Capt. Ebenezer Eastman. He graduated at Harvard College in 1743, and was a man of much intelligence. He died at Concord, Mass., about 1795.

4. For many years Mr. Walker collected more or less of his salary. During the time the town had no legal government, its payment was a voluntary act on the part of his parishioners. The barn alluded to above was taken down in 1830.

Sun. 26. Preached. Baptiz^d Abner——of Jam^s Clements. In the evening visited Aunt Walker.

Mon. 27. Cleared up cold. Set out for Portsmouth. Lodged at Mr. Butler's,[1] Nottingham.

Tues. 28. Very cold, as any ye winter. Went to Dover. Lodged at Capt. Waldron's.[2]

Wed. 29. In company with Mr. Evans[3] went to Portsmouth. In evening visited Col° Atkinson,[4] Dr. Jackson[5] &c.

MARCH.

Thur. 1st day of March. Visited Mr. Treasurer.[6] Afternoon sat out for Newbury. Rained most of the way.

Frid. 2. Rained. Preached Mr. Lowell's[7] lecture &c.

Sat. 3. Dined with Mr. Farnham. Lodged at Mr. Rolfe's.[8] Very cold.

Sun. 4. A. M. Preached for Mr. Tucker.[9] P. M. for Mr. Lowell.

Mon. 5. Sat out homewards. Lodged at Mr. Coffin's.[10]

---

1. Rev. James Butler, pastor of the church of Nottingham from 1758 to 1770.

2. Capt. Richard Waldron, the son of Major Richard Waldron, who was killed by the Indians in 1689.

3. Probably Mr. David Evans, of Concord, a soldier of the French war, and present at the destruction of the village of St. Francois.

4. Hon. Theodore Atkinson, Jr., Secretary of the Province.

5. Dr. Clement Jackson, who died Oct. 10, 1788, aged 82.

6. George Jaffrey, Esq.

7. Rev. John Lowell, minister at Newbury from 1726 to 1767.

8. Possibly Henry Rolfe, Esq., of Newbury, a proprietor of Concord, and father of Col. Benjamin Rolfe, of C.

9. Rev. John Tucker, D. D., pastor of the first church in Newbury, Mass.

10. Rev. Peter Coffin, pastor of East Kingston from 1739 to 1772.

Tues. 6. Snowed. Went to Chester. Lodged at Mr. Flagg's.[1]

Wed. 7. Arrived home comi^s Mr. Josiah Flagg. It cleared up cold. Prince cleaned up 61 bushels Indian corn.

Thur. 8. Visited Aunt Walker, Farrington's child &c. Cleared up some^t, being cool. Moon passed by ye Pleiades &c. Capt. Page's rule failed.

Frid. 9. A number of teams brought me 16 loads of wood,[2] w^h with what I had before made about 20 loads.

Sat. 10. Grew colder. Prince swingled lbs 11 Flax.[3]

Sun. 11. Weather moderated. Preached. Baptiz^d Martha — of Capt. McMillen, and Betty — of Moses Merrill. Voted ye dismission of Ab^m Kimball & wife.

Mon. 13. Attended Town meeting. Concluded to complain to ye King[4] &c. Jos^h Hall and my team sledded 7 loads of maple wood. Continued cold.

---

1. Rev. Ebenezer Flagg, a classmate of Mr. Walker and pastor of the church in Chester from 1736 to 1793.

2. At this time, in addition to his salary, the New Hampshire minister often had furnished to him a stipulated quantity of wood each year.

3. The raising of flax, no longer pursued in New Hampshire, was very common one hundred years ago. It grew like grain, and, when mature, was subjected to several processes to prepare it for use, viz.: 1st, to Pulling, to detach it from the ground. 2d, to Thrashing, by which the seed was separated from the stems. 3d, to Rotting, which destroyed the adhesion of the fibres to one another. 4th, to Breaking, which detached the woody stalk from its fibrous envelope. 5th, to Swingling, which separated the bark and broken stalks from the flax. 6th, to Hatcheling, by which the various impurities were combed from the flax and its fibres straightened.

4. In relation, probably, to the disturbed condition of the affairs of the township, in consequence of the refusal of the provincial government to grant to its inhabitants an act of incorporation.

Tues. 13.   Weather moderated.   Wind South-wardly.   Began to sled dung.   Sledded 9 loads.

Wed. 14.   Weather continued moderate.   Sledded 8 loads dung.

Thur. 15.   Snowed a little A. M.   P. M.   Cleared up wind^y. ——— thawed exceedingly.   Dined with my children at Col° Rolfe's.   Bot. $\frac{1}{4}$ cwt. of Sugar of Capt. McMillen.

Frid. 16.   Prince swingled 12 ℔s. flax.   Weather continued very moderate.

Sat. 17.   A spring like day.   Opened my cabbage vault.[1]   Paid Tim° Bradley 7 dollars on his son Ab^ms. acct.   P. M.   The weather turned up cold.

Sun. 18.   Preached.   Propounded Benjn Hanniford's wife for full communion.   In ye evening visited old Aunt Walker[2] being very bad.

Mon. 19.   A pleasant day.   My men dressed flax.

Tues. 20.   Dined at Col° Rolfes.

Wed. 21.   Went with Prince to get timber for a cart.

Thur. 22.   A pleasant day.   Y^e spring very forward.

Frid. 23.   Drew off 13 barrels of cider, besides about two left on ye lees.   Had a new rum barrel of Mr. Webster towards a barrel of cider he had of me. He also overpaid £5 for a former barrel.

Sat. 24.   Breakfasted at Col° Rolfe's.   Saw a team plowing.   P. M.   Rained somewhat.

Sun. 25.   Preached.   Wife of Nathan Colby owned ye covenant.[3]   Baptized Nathan ——— of Nathan Colby.

---

1. Potatoes and other vegetables were often kept through the winter in pits, dug in the ground, and covered to a sufficient depth with earth to prevent their freezing.

2. Mrs. Margery Bruce Walker, wife or widow of Isaac Walker, one of the original proprietors of Concord and uncle of Mr. Walker.

3. The half way covenant was in use in the Concord church during Mr. Walker's ministry.

Mon. 26.   Prince trimmed my orchard at home.

Tues. 27.   Prince trimmed my Island orchard.[1.] P. M.   Visited Mr. Webster with wife.

Wed. 28.   Went with my men and mended Waternummon's fence in order to keep ye cattle out of ye field.

Thur. 29.   Made up my house lot fence and kept my cattle out of ye field.

Frid. 30.   Misty weather.   Went Mr. Emery to cut timber for a cider mill and press but without success.   P. M.   Visited Col° Rolfe.

Sat. 31.   Capt. Chandler[2] went with Mr. Emery to look out timber for a cider press.   Prince went in his room to roll in ye masts.

N. B.   26th of March sat out 63 young apple trees in a single row beginning next ye road; then sat 2 young plum trees; then five of best winter apples; then 9 of ye spice apple, making 79 in ye whole.

APRIL.

Sun. 1st of April.   Fell a snow about 6 inches deep.   Preached.   Admitted to communion the wife of Benj^a Hanniford.   Baptized Saml —— of Danl Abbot.   P. M.   Cleared off moderate.

Mon. 2.   Set out for Woburn.   Dined at Capt. Stark's.[3]   Lodged at Col° Lovewells.[4]

---

1.   Mr. Walker had an orchard on the west end of Horse Shoe Island.   Three of the apple trees were standing in a tolerable state of preservation as late as 1850.

2.   Capt. John Chandler, one of the original proprietors of Concord, and grandfather of Abiel Chandler, the founder of Chandler School at Hanover.

3.   Capt. John Stark's, at Manchester.

4.   Probably Zaccheus Lovewell, of Dunstable, brother of Capt. John Lovewell of Pigwacket fame.

Tues. 3.   Rained plentifully.   Dined at Mrs.
Blanchards.   Drank tea at Col° Jno. Tyng's.[1]   In
the evening went to Wilmington.   Lodged at my
brother's.[2]

Wed. 4.   Visited at sundry places in Woburn and
went to Roxbury to attend Inferior Court there, but
found 'twas adjourned till Friday.

Thurs. 5.   Visited the President.[3] Mr. Appleton,[4]
Mrs. Brown.   Lodged at Saltmarshes.

Frid. 6.   Went to Roxbury and thence to
Woburn.

Sat. 7.   Went to Wilmington.

Sun. 8.   Preached all day at Wilmington.

Mon. 9.   Sat out for Portsmouth.   Dined at Mr.
Sym's.   Visited at Mr. Barnard's.[5]   Lodged at Capt.
Barnard's, Almsbury.

Tues. 10.   Went to Portsmouth. Visited Mr. ——.

Wed. 11.   Prepared a petition to offer ye General
Court.[6]

Thur. 12.   Presented my petition which was read
in Council.   In the evening went to Kittery.   Took
up note to Sir William Pepperel.   Lodged at Mr.
Steven's.[7]

Frid. 13.   Returned to Portsmouth.   P. M.   The
General Court was adjourned to Tuesday May ye
first.   Set out home.   Lodged at Mr. Sargent's.

Sat. 14.   Arrived home.   It proved a rainy day.

Sun. 15.   Preached A. M.   P. M.   Son Timothy
preached.

1.   In Dunstable.
2.   Deacon Samuel Walker, of Wilmington, Mass.
3.   President Edward Holyoke of Harvard College.
4.   Probably Nathaniel Appleton, Fellow of Harvard College.
5.   Probably Rev. Edward Barnard, pastor of the First Church of
Haverhill, Mass.
6.   For the incorporation of Concord or a renewal of the District
Act.
7.   Rev. Joseph Stevens, of Kittery, Maine.

Mon. 16.   Visited Col° Rolfe.   Pitched ye place for his house.[1]

Tues. 17.   Mr. Hanniford made me a new harrow.

Wed. 18.   Sowed peas at Hale's Point; wheat in Waternummons.

Thurs. 19.   Mr. Virgin sowed rye and peas over ye River.   I sowed on ye Island, and 1 bush^l rye, 1 peck of large peas, 3 pecks of Hotspurs and 5 bush^ls oats.

Frid. 20.   A general Fast.   Preached all day.   A snow fell about 3 inches deep, but a little way in ye woods a foot deep.

Sat. 21.   Cleared up warm.   Sat out about 20 apple trees in ye Island orchard and ye Joel orchard. At night Mr. Scales Junior came here to preach.

Sun. 22.   Mr. Scales Junior preached for me. Baptized John——of John Stevens.

Mon. 23.   Bot 40 young apple trees of Philip Eastman.   Brot y^m home and sat y^m out.

Tues. 24.   Lent Mr. Gale 6 dollars.   Joseph Walker Junior came to live with me a week for £7-10-00.   Set out about 60 young apple trees in ye house lot.   Began to make log fence.   P. M. Deacon Stickney and Mr. Carlton visited me.   Have had 4 or 5 days cold.

Wed. 25.   Made log fence around my young orchard.

Thur. 26.   Nihil memorab^a.

Frid. 27.   Deacon Hall[2] sowed hay seed for me.

Sat. 28.   Harrowed in hay seed.   Bot ½ bushel flaxseed of Edwd Abbot for £3-10-00.

Sun. 29.   Misty weather.   Preached.   Appointed ye sacrament.   Propounded ye wife of Wm Collin for communion.   Proved a rainy night.

---

1.   This house is now occupied by the Rolfe and Rumford Asylum.

2.   Deacon Joseph Hall, the third deacon of the Concord church, 1744-1784.

Mon. 30. Cleared up moderate. Visited Col°
Rolfe.

MAY.

Tues. 1st of May. Wrote a letter to George
Jaffrey Esq. Mended my pasture fence.

Wed. 2. Set out 8 elm trees[1] about my house.

Thur. 3. Plowed my land at yᵉ Middle Interval.

Frid. 4. Went with Capt. Chandler to Col°
Rolfe's to settle about our trial at Portsmouth.

Sat. 5. Sowed a bushel of barley and more than
a bushel of flaxseed and harrowed it in.

Sun. 6. Preached. Administered the Sacrament.
Received the wife of Wm. Coffin to full communion.

Mon. 7. Joseph Walker returned to complete his
month. Worked upon my orchard fence.

Tues. 8. Sold a barrel of cider to Nathᴵ Abbot
for which he is to pay me 1 dollar and ¾.

Wed. 9. We turned yearlings up to Contoocook
plain.

Thur. 10. Prince and John helped Nathᴵ West.
Joseph Walker carted 2 loads of poles to yᵉ cause-
way by Mr. Carter's.

Frid. 11. P. M. We had a fine rain. Things
look finely.

Sat. 12. A pleasant day.

Sun. 13. Preached all day.

Mon. 14. Teams went to Rattle Snake Hill[2] for
rocks for Col° Rolfe. Planted[3] Middle Interval &
Hale's Point.

---

1. Five of these trees are still standing (Dec. 13, 1888), and the
largest has a circumference of 17 feet 6 inches at three feet above the
ground.

2. The ledges of Rattlesnake Hill have afforded stone for building
purposes from the first settlement of Concord. The top sheets were
used at first, most of which were stained. The quarrying methods of
to-day were unknown to the fathers of the town.

3. The first day of May, old style, was considered by the early
farmers of the town as the proper time to plant Indian corn.

Tues. 15.   Furrowed my Island in order for planting. P. M.

Wed. 16.   Set out for Portsmouth.   Lodged at _____.

Thurs. 17.   Went to Portsmouth.   Entered y^e action.   Heard Dunstable and Derry case tried.

Frid. 18.   Post M.   Returned home.   Lodged at Mr. Moody's[1] of New Market.

Sat. 19.   Dined at Mr. Tuck's.[2]   Returned home by Paul Morrill's.   Rained somewhat before I got home.

Sun. 20.   Preached A. M.   P. M. Son preached. Propounded widow Worthen for full communion.

Mon. 21.   Visited Col^o Rolfe.

Tues. 22. Visited wife of Reuben Kimball.   P. M. Attended training.   Paid Joseph Walker £18—05—00 old tenor.

Wed. 23.   Finished the Joel lot fence.

Thur. 24.   Hung ye lower gate.   Visited Col^o Rolfe, being sick.

Frid. 25.   Mr. Nathl Rolfe arrived here.

Sat. 26.   We have advice that ye woman was cleared accused of murdering her child.   Begins to be very dry.

Sun. 27.   Preached.   Admitted the widow Joanna Worthen to full communion.   Baptized John — of Thomas Saltmarsh.

Mon. 28.   Amos Abbot came to make me a cart.

Tues. 29.   Finished my cart and shoeing my sleds.[3]

Wed. 30.   Sent the Col^o molasses within 2 inches and ½ of ye top of ye tub.   Also lb14¼ Sugar bag with it.

---

1.   Rev. John Moody, minister of New Market from 1730 to 1778.

2.   Rev. John Tuck, minister of Epsom from 1761 to 1764.

3.   Mr. Walker's promptness is evidenced by this shoeing of his sleds in May that they may be in readiness for use the next winter.

Thurs. 31.   Col°. Rolfe raised his house.[1]   Capt.
Page and wife came in and lodged with us.

JUNE.

Frid. 1st of June.   Capt. Page returned home.
Went with my chair[2] to yᵉ 11 Lots.[3]

Sat. 2.   Prince began to weed my house lot corn.

Sun. 3.   Preached.   Propounded Nathˡ Merrill,
Samˡ Colby, Benjⁿ Farnham and their wives to own
yᵉ covenant.

Mon. 4.   Joseph Walker set out for Portsmouth.
Continued very dry.   Son Tim° set out for Woburn.
Had hands to weed my Middle Interval corn.

Tues. 5.   Reckoned with Nathˡ West.   Very cold
for yᵉ season of yᵉ year.

Wed. 6.   With daughter Sally visited Col° Rolfe.
Capt Gale arrived here from Haverhill.

Thur. 7.   Continued very dry.   Warm days and
cool nights.

Frid. 8.   At night the witnesses respecting Bowen
&c. returned home.

Sat. 9.   James Abbot Juner[4] arrived from Cowass.

Sun. 10.   Preached.   Nathˡ Merrill & wife owned
yᵉ covenant.

Mon. 11.   Capt Gale & wife dined at our house.
P. M.   The weather suddenly altered.   Yᵉ wind
sprang up at East.

Tues. 12.   A fine and plentiful rain after long drouth.

Wed. 13.   Continued wet.   Transplanted 250
cabbages and cucumbers.   P. M.   Visited Col° Rolfe
being indisposed.

---

1.   Now occupied by the Rolfe and Rumford Asylum.

2.   This chair is said to have been a two wheeled open vehicle,
resembling a chaise with the top removed, and the first carriage on
springs brought to Concord.

3.   A range of 11 lots rear the Concord Bridge.

4.   James Abbot, Jr., was a citizen of Concord as early as March,
1744.

Thurs. 14. They found Thom⁵ Spring missing since Tuesday morning.

Frid. 15. Prince and John work for Webster at his farm.

Sat. 16. At night my men returned from Webster's farm.

Sun. 17. Preached. Sam¹ Colby, Benj" Farnham with their wives owned yᵉ covenant. Baptized Judith — of Eph™ Farnham Juner. and Sarah — of Sam¹ Colby.

Mon. 18. Visited Colᵒ Rolfe.

Tues. 19. Visited Jona. Worthen.

Wed. 20. Mr. Moses Badger visited here : Tarried all night.

Thur. 21. Mr. Paul Burbeen and Sally visited. P. M. Visited Colᵒ Rolfe. Kilᵈ a calf. Lent Mr. Coffin a quarter—wt. ℔s14½ Rained finely all night.

Frid. 22 Rained by showers. Mr. Virgin helped me.

Sat. 23. Mr. Virgin shaved shingles for me.

Sun. 24. Preached all day. Administered yᵉ Sacrament.

Mon. 25. Visited Dr. Carter's.¹ Put my hat into Mr. Kinsman's hand to vend for wʰ he is to make me a new one.

Tues. 26. This day and yᵉ last my men mowed bushes at my upper pasture. Dined at Colᵒ Rolfe's. Pretty hot.

Wed. 27. Dined at Capt. M°Millen's.

Thurs. 28. Mr. Burbeen and sister visited at Capt. Page's. Returned late at night. At night son Timothy returned from Rowley Canady.²

---

1. Dr. Ezra Carter, the first settled physician of Concord.

2. Hon. Timothy Walker was educated for the ministry and preached a short time at Rowley Canada (Rindge), where he declined an invitation to settle. He also preached at other places for different periods but was never settled.

Frid. 29.   Mr Paul Burbeen and sister departed. Very hot.   Josʰ Walker. Samˡ &c. helped me mow bushes.

Sat. 30.   Josʰ Walker. Samˡ &c. mowed bushes for me.

JULY.

Sun. 1.   Preached.   Propounded Danˡ Chandler and wife to own yᵉ covenant.   At night a fine rain.

Mon. 2.   Moulded[1] my Middle Interval corn.

Tues. 3.   A great concourse of people to swear yᵉ military officers.   Dined with Colᵒ Goffe at Capt. McMillen's.   Visited Jona. Worthen.

Wed. 4.   Extremely hot.   P. M.   A remarkable thunder shower.

Thurs. 5.   Simon Trumbull helped fit up my barn.

Frid. 6.   Finished moulding my Island corn.   Set the missing tobacco plants.[2]

Sat. 7.   Sat out for Bakers Town.[3]   Arrived there.

Sun. 8.   Preached at Baker's Town.   Mr. Scales Junior preached for me.   I baptized Esther —— of —— Barber.   In evening I returned home.

Mon. 9.   Began to mow at Hale's Point.   Jos. Walker pd. Simon Trumbull for mending my barn.

Tues. 10.   Reuben Kier came to shingle my barn. Matrᵒ junxi Benjamin Osgood and Miriam Stickney.

Wed. 11.   Continued exceedingly hot weather. Attended Mrs. Osgood's entertainment.

---

1.   Farmers of the olden time designated the three hoeings which they gave their corn as, 1st. Weeding, a simple cutting up of the weeds : 2d. Moulding, the making of a flat hill about the corn plants, dishing towards the centre ; 3d. Hilling, a further elevation of the hill that it might afford support to the stalks.

2.   Tobacco was raised in a small way, for private use, in Concord, down to a time within the memory of persons now living.

3.   Now Salisbury.

Thurs. 12.   Mat° junxi Jacob Waldron and Sarah Abbot.   Reuben Kier finished shingling my barn.

Frid. 13.   Rained hard ye most of ye day. Cleaned out my barn.

Sat. 14.   Hilled my house lot corn.   P. M.   Mowed my Island orchard.   Saml Osgood visited here. Weather continued very dull.

Sun. 15.   Rained.   Preached all day.   Danl Chandler and wife owned ye covenant.

Mon. 16.   Turned my hay.   P. M.   A small shower.

Tues. 17.   Fair but hay dried little.   Got in 2 small loads of hay.

Wed. 18.   A plentiful rain.   Visited Col° Rolfe. At night my cows got into the field.   Cleared up at night.

Thur. 19.   Clouded up P. M. so that hay dried very little.

Frid. 20.   Col. Frie dined with us.   P.   M. Showery.

Sat. 21.   Carted 3 loads of hay.   P. M.   A light shower.

Sun. 22.   Preached.   Col° Frie dined with me. Baptized Molly and Hannah —— of Danl Chandler.

Mon. 23.   Mowed my Island Lot No. 1 with two hands.

Tues. 24.   Finished mowing No. 1.

Wed. 25.   Carted ye hay off No. 1.

Thur. 26.   Hilled my Middle Interval corn.

Frid. 27.   Began to hill my Island corn.

Sat. 28.   Finished hilling.   It has been a very hot week.   No rain but a very growing time.

Sun. 29.   Continued very hot but showery.   Sacramentum administravi.   P. M.   Son Timothy preached.

Mon. 30.   Visited at Jona. Stickneys with other company.

Tues. 31. Went to Contoocook[1] with Mr. Whittemore.[2] Forwarded a composition between Mr. Morrill[3] and Capt. Gerrish. Returned home about 11 o'clock.

AUGUST.

Wed. 1st day of August. Pulled my flax and reaped my winter wheat.

Thur. 2. Reaped winter rye. Equa cont. Very hot weather.

Frid. 3. Very windy in ye morning.

Sat. 4. Carted 15 shocks and ½ of winter rye. Hackd my peas.

Sun. 5. Preached. Baptized Betty — of Reuben Courrier. Propounded Isaac Walker Juner and wife to own ye covenant. Messrs. Paul Burbeen and Thoms Flagg came here the 4th inst.

Mon. 6. Visited at Colo Rolfe's

Tues. 7 A very heavy shower

Wed. 8. A good hay day. Carted two loads from Hale's Point.

Thur. 9. Reaped part of my summer wheat.

Frid. 10. Rained a little A. M. P. M. Cleared away.

Sat. 11. Finished reaping my wheat. Mended fence of Lot No. 1.

Sun. 12. Preached. Baptized Moses — of Benjamin Fifield, and Phebe — of Nathl Abbot Juner. Propounded John Chase and wife to own ye covenant.

Mon. 13. Turned cows into Lot No. 1, ye Island.

Tues. 14. Mowed my grass upon Waternummons Brook.

---

1. Now Boscawen.

2. Rev. Aaron Whittemore, minister of Pembroke from 1737 to 1767.

3. Rev. Robie Morrill, pastor of Boscawen church from Dec. 29, 1761 to Dec. 9, 1766.

Wed. 15. Cows broke into Dan¹ Chandler's corn.

Thur. 16. Mr. Paul Burbeen departed from here.

Frid. 17. Mr. Foster came and dined here. Lent Mr. Webster £6—00—00. cash.

. Sat. 18. Set out with daughter Molly for Canterbury. Dined there.

Sun. 19. Preached at Canterbury. Mr. Foster preached here.

Mon. 20. Cloudy. Bad hay weather.

Tues. 21. A wet season after a considerable drought.

Wed. 22. Spread my flax. Continued showery. Dined at Mr. Emery's.

Thur. 23. Completed my bargain with Mr. Farrington. Sold him my quarter of cider mill for 7 days ½ work. He helped Col° Rolfe on my account one day, so that he owes me 6 days ½ work. Mr. Aaron Stevens was witness to yᵉ bargain and the 6 days ½ work are chalked up above his mantle piece. P. M. Attend Taylors Raising.

Frid. 24. Weather cleared up, having been all this week foul. Fetched 4 bushels ½ Peas from Mr. Virgins.

Sat. 25. A fine hay day. Carted 2 loads of hay.

Sun. 26. Preached all day. Propounded Tim° Chandler and wife to own yᵉ covenant.

Mon. 27. Matrimonio junxi David Evans and Catherine Walker. At night Mr. James Tyng arrived here.

Tues. 28. Visited Major Noyes at Suncook in company with Capt. Walker.

Wed. 29. Carted hay from Hales Point.

Thur. 30. Finished Mowing. At night a smart shower.

Frid. 31. Mr. Nath¹ Rolfe dined with us. Began to fence Hales Point upper lot.

SEPTEMBER.

Sat. 1st of Sepr. Finished haying. Just at night a smart shower.

Sun. 2. Preached A. M. Administered the Sacrament. P. M. Son Timothy preached. Propounded Ezek^l Colby and wife to own ye covenant.

Mon. 3. Children Timothy and Sarah set out for Woburn. Put ye cows in Hales Point.

Tues. 4. Cleaned up 11 bushels peas[1] at Hales Point. and 3 on ye Island.

Wed. 5. Mr. Blaisdell began to work on ye cider mill. Prince helped Col^o Rolfe.

Thurs. 6. Brot cider mill sweep from Rattlesnake Hill. Prince helped Col^o Rolfe.

Frid. 7. Began to frame ye cider mill. At night a pretty hard frost.

Sat. 8. Continues cold. Men worked on ye cider mill.

Sun. 9. Preached. Tim^o Chandler and wife, John Chase and wife, Ezekiel Colby and wife owned ye covenant. Baptized Tabitha and Tim^o — of Tim^o Chandler;—John — of John Chase; Miriam and Ezekiel — of Eze^l Colby.

Mon. 10. Jos. Walker left me for a fortnight to be made up after his three months have expired. N. B. Cider mill expenses are in Diary for 1761 and under ye month of Aug^t.

Tues. 11. Intended to have raised cider mill but was disappointed.

Wed. 12. Rained hard.

Thur. 13. Rain somewhat abated. It has been ye most plentiful rain of any these several years. P. M. Raised ye cider mill.

---

1. Peas were raised in far greater quantities formerly than now. Besides their use for human food, they were ground, mixed with oat meal and fed to swine.

Frid. 14.   Prince helped Col⁰ Rolfe about his chimnies.

Sat. 15.   Thomˢ Flagg came here.   Son Tim⁰ and daughter Sarah returned from Woburn.   Nath¹ Parker and his sister came with them.

Sun. 16.   Preached.   Baptized Caleb — of Stilson Eastman.   This night was a very severe frost.

Mon. 17.   Had a bad cold.   In night was taken with vomiting and purging.

Tues. 18.   Visited at Col⁰ Rolfe's.   Dined with company at Capt. McMillen's.   Signs of a storm.   At night my purging returned somewhat.

Wed. 19.   Set out for Pigwacket.¹   Comitante Capt. McMillen.   Went through Epsom.   Lodged at Capt. Kate's.

Thur. 20.   Breakfasted at Major Titcombs.   Dined at Mr. Stanyan's, and lodged at Kennebunk.

Frid. 21.   Traveled and lodged at a meadow above the Great Falls on Saco River.   Rained somewhat.

Sat. 22.   Arrived at Pigwacket about 10 o'clock.

Sun. 23.   Preached at Pigwacket.   About 45 persons present.

Mon. 24.   Viewed yᵉ interval and yᵉ great meadows.

Tues. 25.   Viewed Lovells Pond.²   Yᵉ great —— went round——.

Wed. 26.   Dined at Mr. Springs.

Thur. 27.   Visited up at yᵉ Mills.   Dined at Nath¹ Merrills.³

---

1.   Pigwacket included the country upon the Saco river now embraced in the towns of Conway and Fryeburg.   Many of their first settlers had been parishioners of Mr. Walker, and thither he was wont to go to visit them and administer to their spiritual wants, until they had pastors settled among them.

2.   The scene of Lovewell's fight with the Indians.

3.   "In the summer of 1763, Mr. Nathaniel Smith moved his family into Fryeburg.   This was the first family of white people which

Frid. 28. Went into the great —— with Col. Frye.

Sat. 29. Visited at Sundry places.

Sun. 30. Preached. Baptized Eliz^h —— of Jedediah Spring.

OCTOBER.

Mon. 1st of October. Set out homeward with a large company. Lodged at Kellog meadow.

Tues. 2. Dined at Stanians. Lodged at Major Titcombs.

Wed. 3. Went through Barrington— Dined at McCleary's at Epsom. Went by Paul Morrill's. Arrived at Reuben Kimballs 5 minutes after 7, in 12 hours to a minute from Major Titcombs.

Thur. 4. Visited at sundry places.

Frid. 5. Husked corn from the Island.

Sat. 6. Rained. Prince helped Benjn Emery husk.

Sun. 7. Preached. Admitted Timo. Walker ye 4th and wife to full communion. Baptized Elizabeth of Aaron Abbot.

Mon. 8. Mr. Hanniford worked upon ye cider press.

Tues. 9. Some small showers. Very warm. John Colby helped Tim^o Chandler.

Wed. 10. Visited Capt. Brown. Comitates, Mrs. Osgood and Capt. McMillen.

Thur. 11. Sowed two bushels of winter rye. Brot a large load of corn from over ye River.

---

erected a habitation in the country vulgarly called Pigwacket. On the 20th November of the same year, Messrs. Samuel Osgood, Moses Ames, John Evans, and Jedediah Spring moved into Fryeburg, from Concord, in New Hampshire, through a rough, hilly country, uninhabited for 50 or 70 miles. Mr. David Evans and Mr. Nathaniel Merrill (then young men) accompanied them as first settlers."—*Introduction to Lovewell's Fight, pp. IV and V., Jan.* 1799.

Frid. 12.   Brot my corn from yᵉ Middle Interval.[1]
At night had a husking.[2]   Mr. Bayley and Mr.
Badger lodged here.

Sat. 13.   Borrowed a barrel of cider of Dr. Carter.

Sun. 14.   Preached all day.   David Gage and
wife owned yᵉ covenant.

Mon. 15.   Placed my corn in yᵉ crib.   Loaded
Mr. Samˡ Clement's—

Tues. 16.   Sent two teams to Capt. Stark for 2
hogsheads of lime.   Made 7 barrels of cider.

Wed. 17.   Made two barrels of water cider.   At
night Mr. Winget and son came and lodged here.

Thur. 18.   Made 12 barrels cider.[3]

Frid. 19.   Rained considerably.   Covered   my
cider press.

Sat. 20.   Made 4 barrels of water cider.   Gave
Lieut. Webster one of them.

Sun. 21.   Preached.   Sacramentum administravi.
Baptized Jeremy of Thomas Stickney.

Mon. 22.   Messrs. Samˡ and Benjⁿ Osgood dined
at our house.

Tues. 23.   Divided the salt &c. which Mr. Clements sent.   I had 1 bushel ———— salt and 1 bushel

---

1.   That part of Concord interval near the Free Bridge.

2.   Huskings have been common in Concord down almost to the
present time.   Both social and economical, they were held in the
evening and often attended by both sexes.   After the husking had
been finished, the company were wont to adjourn from the barn to
the house, where the scene changed from one of work to one of fes-
tivity.

3.   To any one, surprised that the sober parson of a sober New Hampshire parish should make twenty-five barrels of cider in a single year,
it may be said that cider was a common beverage on almost every
farm in the state down to about fifty years ago.   The late Reuben
Abbot, of Concord, once remarked in the hearing of the editor that
he had known his father to put into his cellar sixty barrels in the
fall, which all disappeared in the course of the following twelve
months.

and ¼ rock salt and 3 gal. and ⅔ molasses, worth about £26 N. H. old tenor.

N. B. Deacon Hall paid my son Tim° £5–19–09 Mass. old tenor towards his rates. Son Timothy set out for Rowly Canady.

Wed. 24. Filled up y° lower well and opened y° road for winter that way.

Thur. 25. Mr. Nath Rolfe came up. Benjn Emery returned from Newbury. Prince set out for Woburn.

Frid. 26. A very hard rain.

Sat. 27. Snowed somewhat and very cold for y° season.

Sun. 28. Continued cold. Some squalls of snow. Preached. Baptiz^d Abiel of Tim° Chandler and Anne of Daniel Carter.

Mon. 29. Visited Col° Rolfe. John Colby got a load of candle (wood).[1] Remained cold for y° season.

Tues. 30. Began breaking up. Gilman West helped me and Eben Simonds with two oxen.

Wed. 31. Continued breaking up. Had Gilman West. Eben Simonds and Simon Trumbul with 4 oxen.

NOVEMBER.

Thur. 1st of Novr. Warm for the season. Continued breaking up.

Frid. 2. Heard of ——— arrival in America.

Sat. 3. Cloudy. Moderate weather. Continued breaking up.

Sun. 4. Preached. Baptiz^d Hannah of Eben Hall and Elizabeth of Asa Kimball. Continued moderate.

Mon. 5. Took a plan of Capt. Lovejoy's land.

---

1. This was dry, hard pine wood, very full of pitch, cleft into small pieces, often used instead of a candle, and, at other times, for kindling.

Tues. 6. Mustered my breaking up team. A warm, pleasant day. Brot my corn from ye Middle Interval.

Wed. 7. Plowed down ye Taylor's hill.[1] Son Timothy returned from Boston.

Thur. 8. Rain in night. Thanksgiving.

Frid. 9. Went out to Dunbarton training.

Sat. 10. Capt. Badger[2] and Mr. Foster dined at our house.

Sun. 11. A very rainy day. Mr. Foster preached for me. Administered ye sacrament.

Mon. 12. It cleared up something cold. Capt. Walker's son came and made my lime mortar.

Tues. 13. Set out for Portsmouth. Lodged at Barber's.

Wed. 14. Arrived at Portsmouth. Attended Court.

Thur. 15. P. M. Our case came on and was continued. Lodged at Capt. Folsom's.

Frid. 16. Arrived home. It has been a very cold week.

Sat. 17. Returned Dea^n Hall the 19 Dollars I received of him. On ye Proprietor's account gave McMillen ye receipt from Danl Sherburne for y^e £350 I carried for him. He owes me £2 for getting his deed recorded. P. M. Attended ye funeral of Eben Halls child.

Sun. 18. Preach^d. Baptiz^d Dean Osgood of David Gage. Col^o Frye dined and lodged here.

Mon. 19. A lowery day. Prince brot 7 bushels turnips from Capt. Page's. Brot 600 thin boards from Nathl Abbot's.

Tues. 20. A very rainy day. Boys set ye barn in order.

---

1. "Ye Taylor" was Mr. Walker's neighbor, Mr. James Walker, who was a tailor and lived at the corner of State and Penacook streets.

2. Probably Captain (afterwards General) Joseph Badger, of Gilmanton.

Wed. 21. Cleared up moderate. John Kimball came to help me. Kill^d my old sow. Weig^d 220 ℔s.

Thur. 22. Capt. Walker plaister^d my chamber entry. Pretty cold.

Frid. 23. He plaister^d the long entry.

Sat. 24. He plaister^d the North room. Jno. Kimball helped me four days this week. N. B. Capt. Adams and Mr. Chamberlin here.

Sun. 25. Cloudy. Looked likely for snow. Preach^d all day.

Mon. 26. Capt. Walker began my stone chimney.

Tues. 27. Finished my stone chimney. Weather grew moderate.

Wed. 28. Visited at Enoch Webster's with wife and company. At night Mr. Powers and Scales lodged here. Weather moderate for ye season.

Thur. 29. Tim° Chandler helped me cart dung. Mr. Powers departed for Cowas.

Frid. 30. A snowy day but moderate.

.

Nov. 13. Kil^d a cow. Wt. about 90 per quarter. Hide about 42.

Novr 21 & Decr 3d. } Killed 4 hogs. Wt. about 850.

Decr 3. Killed my sullen heifer. Fore quarters weighed 234 lbs. Sent ye hide to Saml Colby. Wt. 42.

DECEMBER.

Sat. 1st of December. Continued snowing.

Sun. 2. Preach^d. Baptiz^d Barnard — of Tim° Walker 4th. Still snowy weather.

Mon. 3. Still snowy. The snow about 6 or 8 inches deep. Kill^d my 3 hogs and my young cow.

Tues. 4. Dined at Mr. Coffins. P. M. Attended ye funeral of Barnard son of Tim° Walker ye 4th.

Wed. 5.   Capt. Walker laid me two hearths. Jno. Kimball came to help me lay my best room floor.[1]

Thur. 6.   Visited Col° Rolfe.   Helped split a large door stone.

Frid. 7.   Tim° Chandler helped me cart dung. Towards night it rained.

Sat. 8.   A rainy day.   Jno. Kimball finished laying my best room floor.

Sun. 9.   Preach^d all day.   Forgot to propound Eben^r Simonds and wife to own ye covenant.

Mon. 10.   Son Tim° began his school.   Jno. Colby went.

Tues. 11.   Moderate weather.   Spoke to Gale for some staples.

Wed. 12.   Snow fell about 6 inches deep.

Thur. 13.   A very cold N. W. wind.   Silloway died upon ye road near Irvings.

Frid. 14.   Prince was indisposed with a cold.   Mr. West shod my oxen.   Sent Thom^s Spring to school. Jno. Colby has been four days this week.

Sat. 15.   Weather moderate.

Sun. 16.   Preach^d.   Propounded Eben^r Simonds and wife to own ye covenant next Sunday.

Mon. 17.   Sledded two loads of wood out of Waternummons.

Tues. 18.   Carried a load of wood to ye school house and brot, one home at night.   Mr. Stephen Seales came here.   Visited Capt McMillen.

Wed. 19.   Sledded two loads of wood.

Thur. 20.   Snow fell about one foot deep.   Prince cut up my wood at ye school house.

Frid. 21.   John Colby and Jos. Carter brot me

---

1. This floor, which was removed in 1849, was then in good condition. It was made of pitch pine boards, held in place, upon white oak floor timbers, by wrought iron nails, about four inches long. The virtual termination of the Bow Controversy in Dec., 1762, seems to have encouraged Mr. W. to finish his house.

two loads of rails from Jon^a Chase. Dined with my family at Col° Rolfe's. Maj^r Rogers came to Town.

Sat. 22. Major Rogers and Mr. Scales Juner dined here.

Sun. 23. A fine pleasant day. Preach^d all day. Eben^r Simonds and wife owned ye covenant. Baptiz^d—Jona. Stickney and John — of Eben^r Simonds.

Mon. 24. Set out for Portsmouth. Lodged at Mr. Flaggs. Mr. Scales overtook me there.

Tues. 25. Dined at Folsoms, Exeter. Lodged at Folsoms at Greenland.

Wed. 26. An extraordinary storm of snow. Tarried at Greenland. Teams were stopp^d.

Thur. 27. With difficulty we arrived at Portsmouth. The snow so drifted by ye Globe Tavern y^t 'twas with difficulty we worried through.

Frid. 28. A pleasant day but no General Court.

Sat. 29. A second great storm of snow. Drifted very much. Dined at Mr. Cut's.

Sun. 30. Very blustering. Snow flew prodigiously. A. M. Heard Dr. Langdon.[1] P. M Tarried at home.

Mon. 31. Continued cold. No General Court.[2] Visited Dr. Jackson.

[NOTE. Inasmuch as the above mentioned journey to Portsmouth embraced a few days of the following year, the diary of the first twelve days of January 1765, is subjoined.—J. B. W.]

---

1. Rev. Samuel Langdon, D. D., pastor of First Parish in Portsmouth, from 1747 to 1774.

2. Mr. Walker's object in going to Portsmouth at this time, was to obtain of the General Court, if possible, the incorporation of his town or the renewal of the District Act, by which it had once been governed.

1765.

JANUARY.

Jan. 1. Dined at Parson Brown's.[1] Spent ye evening with Dr. Thornton.

Wed. 2. No travelling yet and so continued this week.

Sat. 5. Dined at Mr. Haven's.[2]

Sun. 6. A. M. Preach^d for Mr. Haven. P. M. For Dr. Langdon.

Mon. 7. Y^e General Court met.

Tues. 8. Heard Russells Petition.

Wed. 9. Did little business.

Thur. 10. Left my affairs with Major Blanchard. P. M. Set out homeward. Lodged at Capt Hoits, Stratham.

Frid. 11. Dined with Mr. Stearnes. Lodged at Tiltons.

Sat. 12. Arrived home. Very cold. N. west wind blew hard.

1766.

Sunday 28th September. Preached at Mr. Swan's in Pigwacket. Arrived 25th; lodged at Capt W's.

Monday, 29. Visited and lodged at Mr. Moses Day's. Bap. Judith his daughter.

October 5. Preached at Pigwacket. Bap. Susanna, daught. of — Holt; Barnard, son of Timothy Walker, Jun.; Susanna, daught. of Sam. Osgood; Ann, daught. of Leonard Harriman; Robert, son of David Page; William, son of Jno. Evans; Sarah, daught. of David Evans; Wm., son of Wm. Eaton; Moses, son of Jas. Osgood; Wm., son of Ben. Osgood, 11 bap. at Pigwacket.

---

1. Rev. Arthur Browne, rector of the Episcopal Church, at Portsmouth.

2. Rev. Samuel Haven, D. D., pastor of Second Parish in Portsmouth, from 1752 to 1806.

1780.

w.	m.	1780. JANUARY has 31 days.

7 1 Cold weather begins yᵉ year.

1 2 Continued cold. Preached all day. In yᵉ evening visited the sick son of James Hazeltine.

2 3 Fell a snow of considerable depth. Visited daughter Thompson.[1]

3 4 Coldest weather we have had. Winds high. Snow vastly drifted.

4 5 Weather a little moderated.

5 6 Wind increased. Travelling very difficult.

6 7 Wind continued excessive high. Philip[2] went with a team to Portsmouth.

7 8 Winds yᵉ same. Very cold.

1 9 Weather still yᵉ same. Preached all day.

2 10 Yᵉ first pleasant day for a long time.

3 11 Continued pleasant weather. Mr. Foster arrived from Exeter. being yᵉ first yᵗ arrived since yᵉ turbulent weather.

4 12 Weather continued pleasant.

5 13 The N. W. wind resumed yᵉ ascendency. Married Stephen Hall and Patience Flanders, both of Concord.

6 14 N. W. wind still prevalent.

7 15 Teams yᵗ had been detained below a fortnight by the deep and drifted snow arrived.

1 16 Preached all day. Still very cold.

2 17 Had a very bad cold.

3 18 Visited Daughter Thompson.

4 19 Cloudy, but no snow.

5 20 Cleared up cold.

---

1. Mrs. Sarah Thompson, wife of Benjamin Thompson, afterwards Count Rumford.

2. Philip Abbot, his hired man.

6 21 Visited Daughter Thompson.

7 22 Continued very cold.

1 23 Preached all day. Very cold. The coldest Sunday yᵗ has been for years.

2 24 Son Timothy[1] set out for Boston.

3 25 This and yᵉ preceding day more pleasant than we have had.

4 26 Nothing remarkable.

5 27 Visited at Daughter Thompson's.

6 28 N. W. wind renewed its force.

7 29 Continued very cold.

1 30 Preached all day.

2 31 Perhaps the coldest day we have had yᵉ season.

Account of marriages in January.

13 d. Stephen Hall and Patience Flanders, both of Concord.

FEBRUARY has 29 days.

3 1 Light wind, southerly. Clouded P. M.

4 2 Cleared up. Wind N. W., but not extreme cold.

5 3 A very pleasant day.

6 4 Do.

7 5 The N. W. wind revived with increased vigor.

1 6 Preached all day. In yᵉ evening Col. Hurd advenit.

2 7 A pleasant day.

3 8 A moderate snow, four or five inches deep.

4 9 Cleared up cold. Wind N. W.

5 10 Do.

6 11 Weather a little moderated.

7 12 Had news from yᵉ General Court.

1 13 Preached all day.

---

1. Hon. Timothy Walker.

2 14 Visited at Capt. Roach's.
3 15 Attended y[e] funeral of Mrs. Shute. Began a thaw. Rained chief of y[e] night.
4 16 Mr. Prince preached a lecture here.
5 17 Dined with Mr. Prince[1] at Mr. Kinsman's.
6 18 The thaw much damaged y[e] travelling.
7 19 Attended y[e] funeral of Joseph Clough's child, and baptized Elizabeth, his other daughter.
1 20 Preached and in evening married Samuel Willard and Sarah Thompson, both of Concord.
2 21 Thawy weather. Capt. Kinsman[2] arrived from Boston. No news.
3 22 Visited at Daughter Chandler's.[3]
4 23 Visited at Daughter Thompson's.
5 24 Went to William Brown's and there married John Dobbin and Sarah Brown, both of Chester.
6 25 Cold but not extreme. Son Timothy set out for Exeter.
7 26 Hazy. Likely for a snow.
1 27 Preached at Pembroke. Baptized a daughter of Aaron Whittemore. Do. of John Head. Do. of Nath[l] Lakeman. Mr. Colby[4] preached for me.

---

1. Rev. Joseph Prince, first minister of Barrington.

2. Capt. Aaron Kinsman, of Bow, was an officer of the Revolution who commanded a company in Stark's regiment at Bunker Hill, and served through the whole or a good part of the Revolutionary period. He subsequently resided in Concord, and was highly respected.

3. Mr. Walker's youngest daughter, the widow of Capt. Abiel Chandler, of Concord, who died in 1777. She afterwards married Henry Rolfe, of Concord.

4. Rev. Zaccheus Colby, ordained March 22, 1780, and pastor of the Pembroke church from 1780 to 1803.

2 28 Heard various rumors of ye revolt of Ireland.
3 29 A very pleasant day ends ye month.

Account of marriages in February, viz:

20 D. Samuel Willard and Sarah Thompson, both of Concord.

24 D. John Dobbin and Sarah Brown, both of Chester.

MARCH has 31 days.

4 1 The first, second and third days pleasant.
7 4 Dined at Daughter Thompson's with Sq^r Page.
1 5 The company kept Sabbath here. Preached. Baptized Peter Hazeltine—of Danl Abbot; Abial—of Benj^a Farnum; Saml—of Richard Ayer; Hepzibah—of Jabez Abbot and Betty—Obadiah Hall.
2 6 Dined at Mrs. Osgood's[1] with Sq^r Page. Annual Town Meeting.
3 7 Continued moderate weather.
4 8 Heard pr. Mr. Carlton that Mr. Ingalls from Androscoggin[2] said ye snow had not been above twelve inches deep there this winter.
5 9 Nothing remarkable.
6 10 Last night and to-day fell about six inches snow.
7 11 Cloudy, but no falling weather.
1 12 Preached. Snowed somewhat. Read the letter from Pembroke ch. to assist in ordaining Mr. Colby. The church chose Col. Thomas Stickney and Tim^o Walker, Jr., Esq., delegates.

---

1. Mrs. Hannah Osgood, whose patriotism was as hearty as her hospitality, and who was commonly called "Mother Osgood," kept a well known inn in Concord for many years.

2. About this time many persons emigrated from Concord and settled at Rumford, on the Androscoggin river in Maine.

2	13	A pleasant day.
3	14	Married Alexander Long and Anna Moor of Bow.
4	15	Visited at Mr. Stevens's[1] and Mr. Harris's.[2]
5	16	Married Mr. Nathaniel Rolfe, Junior, and Mrs. Judith Chandler, both of Concord; also James Garvin, Junior, and Sarah Mitchell, both of Bow.
6	17	Nothing remarkable.
7	18	Do.
1	19	Preached all day.
2	20	Nothing remarkable.
3	21	Married Samuel Abbott, Junior, of Pembroke, and Lydia Perrum of Concord.
4	22	Attended ye ordination of Mr. Colby at Pembroke.[3]
5	23	Messrs. Rice and Kelley departed.
6	24	Fell a small flight of snow and hail.
7	25	Cleared up, moderate.
1	26	Preached. Baptized James Osgood — of Jeremiah Abbot.

The last week in March cold blustering weather for ye most part.

Account of marriages in March.

14 D. Alexander Long and Anna Moor, both of Bow.

16 D. Nath¹ Rolfe, Jr., and Judith Chandler, both of Concord.

1. John Stevens, an Englishman, educated at the University of Cambridge, was for many years a trader in Concord. His store stood at the northwest corner of Main and Pleasant streets. In 1777 he was suspected of Toryism and sent to Exeter jail, but was subsequently released by the Legislature. He died in 1792.

2. Robert Harris, for many years a prominent trader and citizen of Concord.

3. Rev. Zaccheus Colby, dismissed May 11, 1803.

(5)

16 D. James Garvin, Jun., and Sarah Mitchell, both of Bow.

21 D. Sam¹ Abbot, Junior, of Pembroke, and Lydia Perrum, both of Concord.

APRIL has thirty days.

7	1	Very cold for yᵉ season. Post brought yᵉ first newspaper we have had.
1	2	Preached all day. Very cold.
2	3	Town meeting —— is adjourned to yᵉ first Monday, July.
3	4	Yᵉ first spring-like day for a good while.
4	5	Weather continued moderate.
5	6	Nothing remarkable.
6	7	Weather grew colder.
7	8	In yᵉ evening hurt my foot badly. N. B. Sat'y yᵉ 8th sowed my first peas.
1	9	Was detained at home by lameness. A. M. A smart rain. Snow up country.
2	10	Cleared up cold. Something of a freshet.
3	11	Continued cold for the season.
4	12	Weather much yᵉ ——. My lameness increased.
5	13	No news from Europe of importance.
6	14	Mr. Foster¹ advenit.
7	15	Daughter Susan pepᵗ.
1	16	Preached. Baptized Betty — of son Timothy Walker.
2	17	A cold rain. Went to mill. Nath¹ Eastman's house was burnt.
3	18	Visited at Daughter Thompson's.
4	19	
5	20	A rainy day.
6	21	Cleared up cold for the season.
7	22	The nurse went away.

---

1. Rev. Abiel Foster, pastor of Canterbury church from 1761 to 1779.

1   23   Weather moderated. Preached. After meeting Sam¹ Davis and wife owned yᵉ covenant. Baptized Robert and Betty, children of do. In yᵉ evening turned up very cold.

2   24   Continued very cold for yᵉ season.

3   25   Weather a little moderated.

4   26   A continental fast. Preached.

5   27   Matᵒ junxⁱ Moses Kimball and Hannah Chase, both of Concord.

6   28   Weather moderated much.

7   29   This week's news gives accᵗ of a large French fleet arrived at Charleston, S. C. Was not attacked yᵉ 7ᵗʰ inst.

1   30   Pleasant weather ends yᵉ month. Preached. Propounded yᵉ Sacrament.

Account of marriages in April.

27 D.   Moses Kimball and Hannah Chase, both of Concord.

MAY has 31 days.

2   1   A cold rain, but moderate.

3   2   Do. The freshet rose, but not high.

4   3   Cleared up but cold for yᵉ season.

5   4   Do.

6   5   The first warm day for some time. Visited at Daughter Thompson's.

7   6   A pleasant day. Post brought yᵉ accᵗ of yᵉ arrival of yᵉ ——.

1   7   Preached. Sacᵐ.

2   8   Rained a little. Catched a violent cold. In yᵉ night was taken with a violent ague fit, with vomiting.

3   9   Was so weak I could scarcely walk. P. M. Catched a bad fall down stairs.

4   10   Grew better. A very warm, pleasant day.

5	11	Turned up cold for the season.
6	12	Weather continued cold for ye season. Mr. Smith of Dartmouth College advenit.[1]
7	13	Weather moderated. Planted my first beans, viz: 8 rows.
1	14	Preached all day.
2	15	Weather continued warm.
3	16	Planted 9 hills of squashes, 9 of cucumbers, and 8 rows of beans, whereof 1 and about ½ were Mr. Kimball's sort.
4	17	Warm, pleasant weather.
5	18	Began to plant Indian corn.
6	19	A remarkable dark day although the clouds appeared thin.
7	20	Finished planting Indian corn. Y^e Post not arrived. The reason not known.
1	21	Preached all day. Began to complain of ye drowth.
2	22	
3	23	Continued warm and dry.
4	24	Saw Capt Mitchell from Androscoggin.
5	25	Visited at daughter Thompson's.
6	26	Heard the good news from Capt. Roach[2] y^t ye Regulars had raised the siege at Charleston, S. C., with considerable loss.
7	27	Had a small, refreshing shower, and another in ye night following.
1	28	Preached; appointed the Sacrament. Baptized Susanna — of Jacob Carter, and Hannah — of Joshua Chandler.
2	29	Son Tim°. set out for Woburn.

---

1. Rev. John Smith, D. D., Professor of Latin and Greek languages.

2. Capt John Roach, a native of Cork, Ireland, came to Concord about 1778. He was a Continental soldier and lived at south end of Main street. He married Elizabeth Rogers after her divorce from her husband, Major Robert Rogers.

3 30   Warm, dry weather.

4 31   Tarried at home almost alone.

Account of marriages in May.

10 D.   John Chandler of Boscawen and Emma Farnum of Concord.

June has 30 days.

5 1   Dined at Mr. Harris's with Mr. Hunt. Matri° junx[i] Daniel Flood of Wear and Sarah Kimball of Concord.

6 2   Visited at daughter Judith's.

7 3   Son Timothy returned from Woburn. N. B. On the evening of the 2d was some frost but did no harm in this neighborhood.

1 4   Preached. Administered y[e] Sacrament.

2 5   Weather moderated.

3 6   Continues warm pleasant weather. Visited at daughter Thompson's.

4 7   Rained moderately most of y[e] day.

5 8   Cleared up cool. A light frost.

6 9   Mr. Kelly advenit.[1] Dined at Mr. Kimball's.[2]

7 10   Warm and some signs of rain.

1 11   Preached all day.

2 12   Nothing remarkable.

3 13   Capt. ———— from Newburyport bro[t] acc[t] y[t] y[e] siege of Charleston was raised.[3]

4 14   Mr. Nath[l] Rogers arrived.

5 15   A moderate rain. Sat out about 140 cabbage plants.

6 16   Cleared up. There was but little rain.

7 17   Something cloudy. Sat out 150 cabbage plants.

---

1. Rev. William Kelly, minister of Warner from 1772 to 1801.
2. Deacon John Kimball.
3. May 12. 1780.

1	18	Preached both parts of ye day.

1 18 Preached both parts of ye day.
2 19 Sat out 150 cabbage plants.
3 20 Some signs of rain.
4 21 In ye night past we had a fine rain.
5 22 Cleared up pretty cool. Heard the news that Charleston. S. C., was taken.
6 23 Warm. growing weather.
7 24 Set out some cabbage plants.
1 25 Preached. Baptized Robert — of Daniel Hall.
2 26 Mr. Woodman[1] and wife advenit.
3 27 Visited at Dr. Green's.[2]
4 28 A fine rain. Mr. Rice[3] advenit.
5 29 Continued raining.
6 30 Heared the French fleet had got possession of Halifax. Finished setting out cabbage plants. Sat in ye whole about 500 or 600. N. B. Agreed with ye Post Rider for half a year's newspapers, beginning ye 28 of June and to end ye 21 of December.

Account of marriages in June.

1 D. Daniel Flood of Wear and Sarah Kimball of Concord.

JULY has 31 days.

7 1 Cleared up warm after a beautiful rain which has mended the prospect of hay, very much.
1 2 Preached. Baptized Sarah — of Stephen Abbot.
2 3 A fine shower.

---

1. Rev. Joseph Woodman the minister of Sanbornton from 1771 to 1806.

2. Dr. Peter Green, who practiced medicine in Concord from 1772 to 1828.

3. Rev. Jacob Rice, minister of Henniker from 1769 to 1782.

3	4	Sat out for Henniker council. Dined at Mr. Fletcher's.[1] Lodged at Capt. How's.
4	5	Met ye other members of ye council at Mr. Rice's.
5	6	Prevailed with ye contending parties to submit their matter to a mutual council. Returned home.
6	7	A very hot day.
7	8	Mr. Hutchinson dined with me.
1	9	Preached. Baptized Jenny — of Asa Kimball.
2	10	Began to mow.
3	11	Cloudy. Rained a little.
4	12	Raked our hay yt was mowed Monday.
5	13	Carted 3 loads of hay.
6	14	Carted 4 loads of hay.
7	15	Cloudy. Signs of rain. Carted 3 loads of hay. Sally Walker[2] returned from Woburn and brought news of ye arrival of ye French fleet at Newport.
1	16	Preached. Propounded Stephen Hall and wife to own ye covenant.
2	17	Carted in ye last of clover, making 15 loads in ye whole.
3	18	A. M. A moderate rain. P. M. Cleared up.
4	19	A good hay day.
5	20	Visited at Mr. Harris's.
6	21	A cool morning, but a pleasant day.
7	22	Remained good hay weather.
1	23	Preached. Remained fair weather.
2	24	Do.
3	25	Do. A small shower in ye afternoon.

1. Rev. Elijah Fletcher, minister of Hopkinton from 1773 to 1786.
2. Afterwards Mrs. Major Daniel Livermore.

4	26	Have had 3 or 4 of the hottest days this season.
5	27	Weather grew a little cooler.
6	28	Weather grew hot again.
7	29	Do.
1	30	Preached. Propounded the sacrament. Stephen Hall's wife owned yᵉ covernant. Baptized Daniel — of Ezra Carter and Moses — of Stephen Hall.
2	31	Visited at daughter Thompson's.

No marriages this month.

AUGUST has 31 days.

3	1	A very warm day.
4	2	Do. P. M. A smart thunder shower.
5	3	Began to reap winter rye.
6	4	Very hot. In yᵉ evening a shower.
7	5	Carted 12 shocks of winter rye. P. M. A small thunder shower.
1	6	Preached. Sac. cel'. Baptized Amos — of Mr. Caleb Chase.[1]
2	7	Went on with reaping our rye.
3	8	Weather very hot about three days.
4	9	Nothing remarkable.
5	10	Finished winter rye harvest. Had about 51 shocks.
6	11	Weather extreme hot.
7	12	Mr. Rawson advenit.
1	13	Mr. Rawson preached for me.
2	14	Visited at Esq. Green's.[2] Finished summer rye harvest. about — shocks. Also stacked our flax.

1. Caleb Chase was town clerk of Concord from 1787 to 1791.

2. Hon. Peter Green was Concord's first lawyer. He commenced practice there in 1767. He held important offices and died in 1798. He was supposed, at times, during the Revolution, to entertain Tory principles, and was consequently unpopular.

3	15	Continued very hot weather.
4	16	There has been 5 or 6 extreme hot days.
5	17	Matr° jux¹ John Straw and Mary Emerson, both of Concord.
6	18	A very plentiful rain.
7	19	Post bro' news of a great mob in London.
1	20	Preached. Weather changed from extreme hot to very cold for yᵉ season.
2	21	Began to reap my Syberian wheat.
3	22	Finished reaping and carting yᵉ Syberian wheat. viz.: 32 shocks.
4	23	Extreme hot.
5	24	Continued yᵉ same.
6	25	The air was cooled by a pleasant breeze.
7	26	Helped Dr. Goss¹ cart his hay.
1	27	Preached. Admitted Nathan Kinsman and wife to full communion.
2	28	Our Androscoggin meeting was adjourned to yᵉ 8 of Sept. next.
3	29	Son Timothy sat out for Exeter.
4	30	Finished yᵉ haying. Yᵉ weather changed to cold for yᵉ season. There has been a long spell of very hot weather.
5	31	Rained a little —— N. B. 22d inst. Sent £200 by yᵉ Post to Henry Gardner. Esq., for taxes for Waterford. 2d Sept. Post bro' me Mr. Gardner's letter yᵗ he had received yᵉ £200 which letter son Timothy has in keeping.

Account of marriages in August.

17 D.   John Straw and Mary Emerson both of Concord.

---

1. Dr. Ebenezer Harnden Goss, who married Mr. Walker's daughter Mary in 1768. He removed to Brunswick, Me., and subsequently to Paris Me.

SEPTEMBER has 30 days.

6	1	Rained somewhat.
7	2	Continued rainy weather.
1	3	A pretty rainy day. Preached. Administered ye sacrament.
2	4	Visited at Daughter Rolfe's.
3	5	Began picking peas.
4	6	Heard ye news of ye re-enforcement of ye French fleet.
5	7	Matr° junx[1] Moses Hacket and Keziah Ladd, both of Goffestown.
6	8	Messrs. Sterns[1] —— Merrill dined here.
7	9	Post brought little news. Spread our flax.
1	10	Preached.
2	11	Visited with Daughter Thompson at Dr. Goss's.
3	12	Nothing remarkable.
4	13	Married Nathan Holt and Sarah Thompson, both of Bow.
5	14	Our Androscoggin ——— sat out.
6	15	Pleasant weather.
7	16	The Post brought no extraordinary news.
1	17	Mr. Fessenden preached for me.
2	18	Went up to Chandler's mill. Contoocook.
3	19	Visited at Mr. Harris's.
4	20	Married William Walker and Eunice Stevens, both of Concord. Made one barrel of cider. Philip Abbot spread his flax.
5	21	Nothing remarkable.
6	22	—— ——. Mr. Fletcher[2] advenit.
7	23	Nothing remarkable.
1	24	Preached and propounded ye sacrament.
2	25	Pleasant weather.
3	26	Philip spread his flax. Mr. Welch adv^t.

1. Rev. Josiah Stearns, minister of Epping from 1758 to 1788.
2. Probably Rev. Elijah Fletcher of Hopkinton.

4	27	A pleasant day.
5	28	Went out to Bow and married John Bayley of Dunbarton and Margaret Hall of Bow.
6	29	Philip Abbot ——— our flax.
7	30	A pleasant day ends ye month.

Account of marriages in September.

7 D.   Moses Hacket and Keziah Ladd, both of Goffes Town.

13 D.   Nathan Holt and Sarah Thompson, both of Bow.

20 D.   Willm Walker and Eunice Stevens, both of Concord.

28 D.   John Bayley of Dunbarton and Margaret Hall of Bow.

OCTOBER has 31 days.

1	1	Preached. Administered ye sacrament. Baptized Ebenezer — of John Farnum and Naomi — of Ephraim Farnum, Junior.
2	2	Went to Flanders' mill with a team.
3	3	Tarried at home.
4	4	Tucker gathered the corn upon Cogswell's[1] lot.
5	5	Took up our flax.
6	6	Finished picking apples.
7	7	Prince plowed at Hale's Point for winter rye.
1	8	Preached all day.
2	9	Nothing extraordinary.
3	10	Visited Daughter Goss.
4	11	Sowed 4 bushels winter rye at Hale's Point.[2]

1. The second lot in the Waternummon's Field in Concord.

2. Hale's Point, as may be seen by consulting the map of the Concord interval, found in the records of the proprietors, and also in Bouton's History of Concord, page 125, was in 1780 on the west side of the Merrimack river. It is now upon the east side, having been cut off by a freshet in January, 1828.

5	12	Married Bruce Walker and Mehitabel Courier, both of Concord.
6	13	Rained moderately.
7	14	Visited Mr. Hunt at Mr. Harris's.
1	15	Preached. Baptized Betty — of Nath¹ Currier.
2	16	Rained, and as we hear. snow up country.
3	17	Went on with Indian Harvest.
4	18	Began making cider. Made 6 barrels and ½.
5	19	Made 3 barrels water cider.¹
6	20	The town was assembled to raise men to resist yᵉ enemy at Cowos.
7	21	Finished making cider, having made 13 barrels cider and upwards of 5 of water cider.
1	22	Preached. Baptized Hetty — of Majᵣ Jonathan Hale.
2	23	Visited at Daughter Thompson's.
3	24	Finished gathering corn.
4	25	Finished husking.
5	26	Visited at Mr. Harris's.
6	27	Visited at Daughter Goss's. A remarkable eclipse of the sun about noon.
7	28	Mr. Fletcher advenit in his way to Canterbury.
1	29	Yᵉ most plentiful rain we have had for a long time. Preached all day.
2	30	Went to Flanders' mill and to yᵉ clothier.²
3	31	Went again to Flanders' mill.

————

Account of marriages in October.

12 D. Bruce Walker and Mehitable Courier, both of Concord.

————

1. "Water cider" was a weak cider, made by watering the pumice, after the ordinary pressing. It was usually drank before that of the best quality.

2. Much of the woolen cloth worn at this time was spun and woven on the farm and dressed at a clothier's mill.

November has 30 days.

4	1	A cold snow storm. Snow fell about two inches.
5	2	Cleared up cold for ye season.
6	3	Continued cold.
7	4	The post brought no remarkable news.
1	5	Preached. Baptized John Bucklee — of Peter Green. Esq.
2	6	Continued cold.
3	7	Married Alexander Simpson of Wenham and Molly Rogers of Bow.
4	8	Returned home from Bow.
5	9	Married Jonathan Runnells and Dorothy Dimon. both of Concord.
6	10	Continued cold.
7	11	Post bro't considerable news both from ye Southward and from Europe.
1	12	Preached A. M. P. M. Mr. Sweat preached.
2	13	A light snow y^t part covered ye ground.
3	14	Cleared up moderate.
4	15	Continued pleasant weather.
5	16	Do.
6	17	Do.
7	18	A. M. Set out for Hopkinton. Y^e weather misty. P. M. Rained moderate.
1	19	Preached at Hopkinton. Mr. Fletcher preached for me A. M. P. M. Mr. Ward.[1] The most plentiful rain we have had for a long time. In ye evening went to Capt Page's.
2	20	A pleasant day. Returned home.
3	21	Do. The frost near out of ye ground.
4	22	Fell a snow about 6 inches deep.
5	23	Cleared up moderate. Visited at Mr. Harris's.

1. Rev. Nathan Ward, minister of Plymouth from 1765 to 1798.

6	24	Moderate weather.
7	25	A considerable rain.
1	26	Preached all day.
2	27	Married Tappan Evans of Warner and Abigail Merrill of Concord.
3	28	The post arrived, bro't the good news of the arrival of ye French fleet off Georgia.
4	29	A summer-like day. Dug 10 bushels of parsnips. Had dug 8 before.
5	30	Cloudy, dull weather ends ye month.

Account of marriages in November.

7 D.   Alexander Simpson of Wenham and Molly Rogers of Bow.

9 D.   Jonathan Runnells and Dorothy Dimond, both of Concord.

27 D.   Tappan Evans of Warner and Abigail Merrill of Concord.

DECEMBER has 31 days.

6	1	A severe cold day begins ye month.
7	2	Continues very cold. Weather much ye same.
1	3	Preached all day.
2	4	Visited down in town.
3	5	Weather very cold.
4	6	Nothing remarkable.
5	7	A continental annual Thanksgiving.
6	8	Worked upon my bridge.
7	9	Signs of foul weather.
1	10	A soaking rain. Preached all day.
2	11	Nothing remarkable.
3	12	Visited at Daughter Judith Rolfe's.
4	13	Visited at Daughter Thompson's and Major Hale's.
5	14	Married Timothy Hall of Concord and Anna Foster of Bow.

6 15 The post called here in his way to Boston.
7 16 Mr. Allen with one hand called here.
1 17 Preached. Baptized Hubbard Carter — of Daniel Gale.
2 18 Wrote a petition to have our incorporation mended.
3 19 A rainy day. Visited at Capt. Kinsman's.
4 20 A cold day.
5 21 Visited at Mr. Harris's.
6 22 Very cold weather.
7 23 A moderate snow.
1 24 Continued snowing a little.
2 25 Snow fell about one foot deep.
3 26 Cleared up cold. Snow drifted.
4 27 Continued cold and windy.
5 28 West shod our oxen.
6 29 The first day of ye teams hauling wood out ye woods.
7 30 Continued cold but not windy.
1 31 Weather moderate. Preached all day.

———

Account of marriages in December.

14 D.   Timo Hall of Concord and Anna Foster of Bow.

INDEX.

L & C.

www.ingramcontent.com/pod-product-compliance
Lightning Source LLC
Chambersburg PA
CBHW030000030726
47499CB00008B/2837